FIGHT FOR FREEDOM

FIGHT
FOR FREEDOM

An Adventure of World War II

by RICHARD ARMSTRONG

illustrations by Don Lambo

DAVID McKAY COMPANY, Inc.　　　New York

SECOND PRINTING, FEBRUARY 1968

First American Edition, Published by
David McKay Company, Inc., 1966

LIBRARY OF CONGRESS CATALOG CARD NUMBER: 66-22208

MANUFACTURED IN THE UNITED STATES OF AMERICA
VAN REES PRESS • NEW YORK
Typography by Charles M. Todd

AUTHOR'S NOTE

ALTHOUGH the characters in it are imaginary this story is based on recorded fact. *Greece and Crete 1941* by C. Buckley, to which book I am indebted for the details of the Battle of Crete, speaks of the escape of various groups of men under their own steam after the island was lost; *Merchant-men at War, The Official Story of the Merchant Navy: 1939–1944* mentions briefly Cadet J. H. Dobson, B.E.M. who on his first voyage was captured by the Germans in Crete, escaped, fought through the retreat and navigated a landing craft full of troops to Egypt; and *The Mediterranean Fleet, Greece to Tripoli, The Admiralty Account of Naval Operations April 1941 to January 1943* tells in two terse pages how Major R. Garrett of the Royal Marines took another landing craft from Sphakia across to Africa. Freely adapting and enlarging these bald facts, I have telescoped them with other isolated incidents to make what I hope is a coherent story about the ability of the human spirit to triumph over defeat which was so powerfully demonstrated in the Battle of Crete and its aftermath.

FIGHT FOR FREEDOM

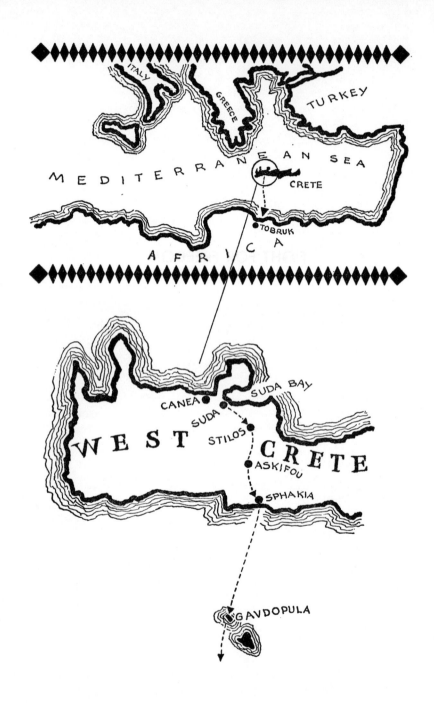

CHAPTER 1

ON THE evening of Tuesday the 27th of May 1941, Stan Bryant crouched in the mouth of a shallow cave on the coast of Crete and watched a wave of Heinkels come in from the north across Suda Bay. They came in fast and low, so low the swastikas on their wing tips looked enormous and the beach quivered with the drumming of their engines. As they passed he saw the doors in their big bellies open and the bombs leave the racks to fall a split second later on the heap of rubble that had once been Canea, the capital city of the island. Then came the noise of them exploding: a crumping, shattering roar that blotted out the throb of the planes and all the lesser sounds of battle. The cliff, the very bones of the island seemed to rock with the blast and a little shower of rubble shook down from the low roof of the cave. Behind Stan, the Skipper spat out a mouthful of chalk dust and swore softly under his breath.

"Come farther back, son," he said. "And don't move. The next lot will be Messerschmitts machine-gunning and those Jerry pilots have eyes like hawks."

"Okay, sir. I'll watch it." Stan grinned reassuringly. "How's it going?"

"Difficult to say." The Skipper, who had just returned along the beach from H.Q. on the outskirts of Suda, fished his stinking old briar out of the breast pocket of his filthy shirt and drew on it thoughtfully for a moment. "The field telegraph isn't functioning any more and the only means of communication is by messenger—when they can get through."

"But you got some idea?"

"Yes, for what it's worth. I'll show you." The Old Man rolled over on to his side, and picking up a splinter of driftwood, etched a rough plan on a patch of smooth sand, then continued. "Here's Suda and the western end of the bay. And here's the coast road, running into what's left of Canea about two miles away and then on towards Maleme. A mile or so beyond Canea the road crosses the Mournies Stream. It runs down out of the hills and north through the olive groves to the sea. Something like this." He paused to draw in the stream. "So far as I can make out, we're holding him there."

"You're not very happy about it?"

"I'm not." The Skipper shook his gray head and sucked in his lips as if he was tasting something bitter. "We've had it, son. I guessed it last night when the order came to evacuate the dock area."

"But you said we were holding."

"For the moment, yes. But without air support it's only a question of time." The Skipper sucked at his cold pipe for a moment in silence, then went on in a hard, dry voice. "No, we've got to face it, my boy. The battle for Crete is over and we're on the losing end."

Stan stared at him blankly, then looked away across the

bay, trying to work out just what his words meant, what the implications of them were for him personally.

Strictly speaking he had no right to be mixed up in the Battle of Crete at all, or any other battle if it came to that. He was neither soldier, airman nor fighting sailor but a Merchant Navy apprentice which made him by all the rules of war a non-combatant. And besides this, he was too young to bear arms anyhow. The kind of war Germany had loosed on the world in September 1939, however, knew no rules and honored no conventions. It was total war and involved everybody, male or female, young or old, who was unlucky enough to get in its way. That was what had happened to Stan. He had got in the way.

When it began he was only a month or so past his sixteenth birthday and right at the start of his seafaring career. A few days before the tanks began to roll outwards across the frontiers of Germany, he had shipped aboard the motor vessel *Kyle*, a small, fast cargo-liner bound for the States and she was still on passage across the North Atlantic when the news broke that Europe was at war again.

Like everybody else outside Germany Stan was shocked but he didn't see it affecting himself very much. Not then. It was all too far off and besides, the general opinion at the time was that it would be over by Christmas.

Of course it wasn't over by Christmas—not that Christmas, nor the next, nor even the one after that; and it began to affect Stan's life right from the word go. Instead of reloading in the States for home according to schedule, the *Kyle* shipped a cargo of lumber to the Cape, then went on to India and southeast from there to Australia. By this time the voyage which should have lasted only days was being measured in months and the end of it wasn't even

in sight. Stan didn't much mind—not just then. He was
getting around and he was learning, which was precisely
what he had come to sea for. But when she went north
and west from Australia to the Persian Gulf, then to India
and back to the States again via the Cape, he began to
feel a little homesick which didn't do him any good at all.
He had to wear it however and after twelve months out
he was still wearing it. She was lying in Rio then, loading
for New Orleans, and the days were dragging their feet.
After discharging at New Orleans she lay six weary weeks
at anchor in the Mississippi waiting for orders which,
when they came, sent her round the Cape once more and
through the Suez Canal to Alexandria.

Although the German U-boats and surface raiders were
active during this period all over the North and South
Atlantic, the *Kyle* by some lucky chance escaped attack
and when she reached Egypt in the spring of 1941, Stan
hadn't yet heard a single shot fired in earnest. He had got
on with the business of learning his trade, and the war had
remained remote. But it caught up with him in Alex and
he'd heard and seen plenty since.

These were the dark days of retreat. The great war
machine of Germany had continued to roll outwards
across Europe until it flaunted its swastika emblem from
the North Cape to the Mediterranean and from the English Channel to the Russian Steppes. Greece had gone at
the end of April, leaving the forces of freedom a last precarious toe-hold on the island of Crete, sixty miles south
of the mainland.

And now, according to the Skipper, this too was lost.
He couldn't believe it; or maybe he just didn't want to.

"It doesn't make sense," he protested; then the Messerschmitts started to come in over the hill. They flew in a

double line, swooping down till they almost skimmed the water and the stuttering chatter of their machine guns rose above the blasting roar of the engines to merge with the flat spang of mortar shells and the sharp crackle of rifle fire from the edge of the town. There was no opposition, not even a single "ack-ack" battery, let alone a fighter to challenge them and as he hugged the gravel beach Stan thought back over the last ten days and tried to stop kidding himself.

Crete is about one hundred and sixty miles long and from seven to thirty-five miles wide. Mountain ranges rising to eight thousand feet run east and west along the length of it, and it fronts the sea with towering cliffs most of the way round its coast line. Apart from an odd strip of shingle beach with a fishing village huddled between it and the foot of the cliff there is nothing remotely resembling a harbor in the south and all the main centers of population—Canea, Suda, Retimo and Heraklion—are in the north. They are linked by the only reasonable road the island can boast of, and off it the country is a nightmare of rocky ridges and deep ravines. From the military point of view it was a pain in the neck but enormously important, for whoever held it, dominated the sea routes through the eastern Mediterranean.

Because of this the decision was made to hold Crete, and every available ship was thrown into the task of reinforcing, equipping and supplying its garrison.

That was where Stan came in. One of those ships was the *Kyle*. She had sailed from Alex early in the month as part of a fast convoy bound for the naval base at Suda Bay.

Rugged just about describes what followed. The British Navy had control of the sea around the island, but the German *Luftwaffe* operating from newly captured airfields in Greece commanded the air above it and they fairly plastered the little convoys and their powerful escorts. Many were lost before they ever saw the island and even those which got through to Suda Bay, the *Kyle* among them, were dive-bombed and machine-gunned incessantly as they lay alongside discharging their cargoes of food, guns and ammunition.

Ship after ship was sunk or set on fire at her moorings, and from where he lay now, Stan could see the masts or blasted upper-works of thirteen protruding from the waters of the bay. One was a tanker. She was still burning and the smoke from her hung like a low black cloud between him and the setting sun. Beyond her and almost completely submerged lay all that was left of the *Kyle*. On the morning of the 15th she had been dive-bombed by a string of Stukas coming unseen out of the sunrise. One direct hit abaft the main mast had blown off her stern and another in the engine room finished the job. Many of her crew were killed in the attack but those who survived, including Stan and the Skipper, stayed on in the dock area, working as stevedores. They didn't feel particularly heroic about it; but there was nowhere else to go and nothing else to do and handling cargo was their line. So they stuck it.

And now it became more rugged than ever; but even so, given time, the island could have been made as impregnable as Gibraltar. Time was denied them, however, and of all the things they hadn't got, which included air cover, heavy guns and tank reinforcements, time was probably the most important. Only three weeks after the evacuation of Greece, the Germans mounted their attack and the battle was on.

It began on the morning of May 20th with an all-out bombardment from the air followed by the landing of air-borne troops. The immediate objectives were the airfields at Maleme, Canea, Retimo and Heraklion, and wave after wave of troop-carriers and gliders came in to them from the north. They carried picked men, specially trained for the job and filled with fanatical courage or maybe just puffed-up and cock-a-hoop with a long succession of easy victories and eager to chalk up another one. It turned out to be anything but a piece of cake for them. Hundreds were killed or captured as they drifted down by parachute or scrambled out of the crash-landed gliders and at the end of the first day, they had all been pretty well mopped up except at Maleme which is in the extreme west of the island. There, at a fantastic cost in men and machines, a foothold was gained on the disused airfield and by night-fall planes were landing on it with reinforcements and equipment at something like three-minute intervals. Except for small-arms fire they came in unchallenged like underground trains in the rush hour, because the nearest fighter-aircraft bases were in North Africa and too far off to provide air support to the Allied ground forces.

Next day the German hold on Maleme was consolidated and the drive eastwards along the coast road began.

This much Stan knew for sure; but that was six days ago and since then news had been scarce, fragmentary and unreliable. He knew vaguely that the defending force, made up of British, Australian, New Zealand and Greek troops, had been heavily engaged throughout the period; that they had been slowly driven back along the road, fighting desperately for every inch of it and every tree and boulder along its length. But he also knew for sure that though most of the dock workers and base personnel had been withdrawn from the Suda Bay area the previous night, a mine-layer had landed reinforcements there before dawn; and now his mind clutched at this fact as a drowning man grabs at a straw.

"What about the reinforcements that landed last night, sir?" he demanded, turning back to the Skipper. "Won't they make a difference?"

"Only to the price Jerry has to pay for his victory."

"But they're Marine Commandos!" protested Stan. "I spoke to some of them."

"If they were giants, if every one of them was a Hercules it still wouldn't affect the issue. They're too few and too late. The general withdrawal has already begun."

"I can't believe it! And besides there's the navy. That mine-layer coming in last night proves we've still got command of the sea and they can't take the island while we control the approaches to it. It doesn't add up."

"It will when you put in all the facts. The navy's paying a terrible price in ships and men for that control you talk about and it can't go on much longer. But apart altogether from that, the situation's just about as grim as it can be." The Skipper leaned forward. "Look, navy or no navy, for the last six days Jerry's been pouring in a steady stream of fresh troops and heavier equipment. He's built up a tremendously powerful force and our own fellows are battle weary; they're worn out from lack of sleep, short of food and ammo and hopelessly outnumbered and outgunned into the bargain. The Jerries are still coming and we can't do a thing to stop them. Listen to those Messerschmitts! There'll be another cloud of Heinkels or maybe Stukas behind them. No, son. We'd be crazy to fool ourselves about it. With no air cover, it's been a losing battle for us from the start."

Stan stared at the Skipper for a moment. He had seen him grow dirty, unshaven and haggard with weariness during the last six days and that didn't seem to matter much the way things were; but now, behind the tiredness in his red-rimmed eyes he saw something else: hopelessness, the sadness of defeat. He had never encountered it before. It brought a lump into his throat he couldn't swallow; it frightened and bewildered him, and abruptly he turned away to look out again across the bay.

Although he was coming up for eighteen and had grown tall and strong for his age and learned a great deal about life and the living of it in the last two years, in many ways he was still the boy who had shipped aboard the *Kyle* in the summer of 1939. His blue eyes still held a wondering, trusting look; his square-jawed face was flayed red with sun and wind but remained unlined and scarcely needed a razor yet; and though his shoulders had grown broad they had never felt the burden of responsibility. The Skipper had always carried that; he made the decisions and issued the orders and Stan had grown used to relying on him. So what he saw now in the Old Man's face shook him to the core, and quite suddenly, as he watched the last of the Messerschmitts make its run in, he realized just what they were up against. The Skipper was right. Stan both knew it and accepted it now. But it still wasn't easy, and with the knowledge in his eyes he turned back to the Old Man.

"What are we going to do, sir?" he asked.

"That's the problem, son." The Skipper squared off his shoulders and stuck out his jaw as if facing up to it. "All that's left now is evacuation. The question is how many can be got away and how many must be left to spend the rest of the war as prisoners behind the wire. The plan's been worked out and I've got the bones of it. Trouble is there's no hope of lifting anybody off the north coast, and in the south there's only one point that can be approached from seaward. That's this little fishing village called Sphakia."

"But that means retreating across the mountains!"

"That's right. It's the only way open."

"Okay then. When do we start? Where's the assembly point?"

"There isn't one. Not for us. We're non-combatants—civilians."

Stan scowled in the effort to understand what the Skipper was driving at. "What difference does that make, sir?"

"All the difference in the world. The road to Sphakia is open now but we don't know how long it will stay that way, only that it won't be long enough to get everybody out. That's for sure."

"I still don't see——"

"There's a war on, son," interrupted the Skipper. "Priority will be given to fighting troops. It must be. As civilians we don't count in this situation. Not so you'd notice."

Stan saw the logic of this and he understood now the look in the Old Man's eyes; but that didn't make it any easier to take. "You don't mean we've got to sit here till a bunch of Jerries come along to put us in the bag!"

"That's about the size of it, son." The Skipper sighed. "One consolation is it can't be any worse than what we've been through. At least we'll get some sort of regular grub and a place to sleep; and we won't be bombed and machine-gunned all day and night. I suppose they'll keep us here till they've got the place cleaned up then ship us to Germany——"

"But the war might last another two years yet!"

"Three, I reckon. At least. More likely five the way it's going."

"Five years!" Stan stared at the Skipper in horror. Five years in a prison camp, doing nothing, getting nowhere! Five years on the shelf, eating his heart out in forced idleness or being pushed around—doing things without purpose or meaning! Five years of emptiness and boredom just when the tide of life was running at the flood in him! He'd be nearly twenty-three at the end of it and his way still to make—if he didn't go bonkers in the meantime which seemed the likeliest thing to happen. It was unthinkable, and suddenly his mind was made up. He wasn't standing for it. Not at any price.

"Look, sir!" he said. "The people who got away from Suda last night; what orders did they have?"

"They were instructed to make their way to Sphakia."

"Well, those instructions applied to us too, didn't they?"

"They did, I suppose." The Skipper frowned. "All base personnel and non-combatant elements, the order said. Only somebody had to stay behind to clear up."

"I know. And that somebody was us. But we've done it now and the order still stands."

The Skipper agreed the order had never been canceled and there was no possibility now of any new one being issued to them; but he pointed out the whole idea of getting the unorganized dockers and base workers out of the area the previous night had been to get the single narrow road across the mountains clear of stragglers before the retreat began.

"You're thinking we should try to get out on our own," he said. "And I don't blame you. But we'd never make it; never get through. We'd get all tangled up in the withdrawal and only complicate things for those in control. It can't be done, son. Let's make up our minds to it."

Stan stuck out his jaw. "Not while I can still push one

foot in front of the other. I'm not suggesting we should take the road——"

"But there's no other way, boy!"

"There's the whole of Crete on either side of it. We can go across country, keeping as close to the road as possible without getting on to it."

"I see what you mean. And even if we lost the road completely we'd be bound to fetch so long as we kept on heading south. Once we reached the coast it would be easy enough to find Sphakia." The Skipper twisted up his face and scratched savagely at his tangle of beard. "It's terrible country, but I suppose it could be done, if we lasted."

"Even if we got killed in the attempt, it would be worthwhile; better than sitting here waiting for Jerry to pick us up and shove us in the cooler anyhow."

For maybe half a minute the Skipper stared at Stan without speaking. The sad, lost look had gone from the back of his eyes. They were fierce again, glinting under their shaggy brows as he considered the chances, the dangers and the sheer physical hardship taking to the mountains would involve and measured Stan against them. Then he too made up his mind.

"Right!" he snapped. "We'll start at dusk."

And as the next wave of bombers came roaring in over the hill, they got down to preparing themselves as far as possible for the hazardous journey towards freedom.

CHAPTER **2**

IN CRETE at this time a hole in the ground such as a cave
was the only place in which a fellow could expect to
survive long enough to see his next birthday, and Stan had
gone to earth in this one with the Skipper after the Stukas
blasted the *Kyle* out of existence. But all their gear had
been lost with the ship. They had got clear of her with
nothing except whole hides and what they stood up in,
which was shoes, khaki-drill shirts and pants, tin hats
and, in Stan's case, a sea-stained blue battle-blouse and a
sheath-knife. During their stay in the cave they had acquired no more than a couple of water-bottles, a jerry-can
of fresh water to fill them from and a haversack. In this
last item Stan, who was endowed with the appetite of a
horse, had from time to time stowed an assortment of
ship's biscuits, chocolate and boiled sweets, like a squirrel
in days of plenty storing nuts for the winter to come.

In these circumstances, the question of what to leave
and what to take on their trip across the mountains didn't
arise. They refilled their water-bottles and when Stan had
slung the haversack across his shoulder and settled the

sheath-knife at the back of his belt under the battle-blouse, they were ready to go. But although the sun had set now and the light was fading fast, the bombers were still plastering the area between Suda and Canea and the Skipper judged it wise to wait for a lull.

"One thing I'm glad of," he said between sucks at his cold pipe. "We've both got a decent pair of stout walking shoes, though I'm willing to bet there won't be much of them left but the lace-holes by the time we fetch Sphakia. If we ever get so far, that is."

"Oh we'll get there all right, sir. We've only got to keep going."

"Yes, that's right; but don't get too cocky about it, son. It won't be any picnic, and we'll be lucky if we do it in under three days."

"Three days!" Stan was incredulous. "But the whole island's only thirty-five miles across at its widest! I've done twenty in a day before now and hardly felt tired at the end of it."

"Maybe you have; but in a different kind of country and under slightly different circumstances. This one's a nightmare once you leave the coast road and there won't be any pull-in along the way where you can get a cup of coffee and a doughnut and rest with your feet up. And that's saying nothing about Jerry and his Messerschmitts. Once he tumbles to what's going on, it won't be healthy to move on the open hillside during daylight."

Up to this point Stan hadn't even stopped to think about what they were up against. With the prospect of spending the next three or more years rotting behind the wire staring him in the face, what he had to do to get out of it didn't seem to matter; just so long as he did get out of it. But now he began to realize that though keeping out of

the cage might be simple, there wouldn't be much percentage in it for him unless he also kept alive and all in
one piece. And with mountains to climb in the dark and
hawk-eyed Jerry pilots to dodge in the daytime, with
nowhere to shelter, no blankets and no food except what
he carried in his haversack, this was going to be anything
but simple.

"You've got no idea of the layout of the country, I suppose?" asked the Skipper.

Stan shook his head. "Only that Sphakia lies south of
Suda with the mountains between."

"I drove over it about a week ago and know it pretty
well; but that wouldn't be much help if you got adrift and
it worries me. We could so easily lose each other in the
dark. Look!" With a sweep of his hand across the patch of
sand, the Old Man obliterated the plan he had drawn of
the Suda area and swiftly etched in another. "This will
give you some sort of picture of the road and the main
points along it."

"Does it matter all that much?" asked Stan. "I thought
we'd decided to keep clear of the road."

"So we shall but it's still important because it's the only
feature we can get our bearings from. Not only that but
it gives us a direct line on Sphakia."

"I see what you mean, sir. So long as we keep to the
westward of it we're okay; but if we blundered across it
without knowing and got to the eastward, we'd be properly
bushed and might never find the place."

"That's about the size of it; so get as much of this as
you can into your head."

Stan leaned forward and studied the rough map in the
dying light while the Skipper filled in the details for him.

The road to Sphakia, it seemed, branched off the main

coast road at a place called Beritiana some distance east of Suda. From there it wound tortuously in a general southerly direction and climbing all the time to the next place name which was Stilos, then veered slightly eastwards to Neon Khorion. After passing through this village, and still climbing, it straightened out somewhat and ran dead south, but not for long, turning southeast just short of Babalikhani, then swinging abruptly south again three or four miles beyond it. There was a fork at this big bend which went on to Retimo, and from this point the road to Sphakia, being less important and less frequently used, became correspondingly more rugged and lonely as it fought its twisted way to the crest of the main ridge, over seven thousand feet above sea level. There were occasional high plateaus covered with olive trees and the odd lost farmstead tucked away in the mouth of a side valley; but in the main the mountain was wild and desolate, murderously stony and arid, and chopped up into a fantastic confusion of deep ravines and rocky defiles. Beyond and below the crest and with about a third of the distance still to cover, the road came to a vast green fertile plain which the Skipper called the Askifou Saucer. The shape of it Stan gathered was saucer-like and the road ran round the rim and then plunged through a succession of gorges southwards towards the brink of the five-hundred-foot cliffs under which Sphakia lay. There were only two more place names of importance after passing Askifou. They were Imvros and Vitsilokoumos.

"Got all that, do you think?" demanded the Skipper.

"More or less, sir. Vitsilokoumos!" Stan rolled the word on his tongue as if tasting it. "They've got some queer names, I must say."

"It's a queer country and I for one won't be sorry to see the back of it."

The last of the bombers had now made its run and the mortaring seemed to have stopped too. Except for a thin crackle of rifle fire in the direction of Canea, a sudden silence lay over Suda Bay. The Skipper lifted his head, listening.

"Looks like this is our cue," he said and grabbed his water-bottle.

Scrambling out of the cave, they set off along the beach and presently were picking their way through the ruins of Suda towards the coast road. In the last fortnight they had grown accustomed to moving about in the darkness and this facility was going to stand them in good stead during the next few nights, but for the moment there was still a fair amount of light in the open—enough at least to show them what the war had done to the town. It wasn't pretty to see. The place seemed encased in a frozen silence on which the tramp and shuffle of feet sounded painfully loud. There was no sign of life. It looked as if it had been deserted for a thousand years but was still haunted by the ghosts of broken hopes and shattered dreams. They were glad to get out of it.

The coast road when they reached it presented a very different picture. It was choked with troops, transport and guns, streaming eastward and though all civilian and non-combatant elements were supposed to have evacuated the area twenty-four hours before, there were unorganized stragglers stumbling among the marching soldiers in considerable numbers. They didn't help at all. And after a week of almost incessant bombing the surface they traveled on was pitted with craters, and the column in consequence moved slowly with frequent involuntary halts.

This was the retreat and the sight of it was even more painful than the ruin of Suda had been. The column was grim faced and voiceless. Except for the sound of its many feet, and now and then a truck revving up as it negotiated a tricky spot in the road, it moved in a numbed silence. Stan and the Skipper watched it, looking for a break that would allow them to cross the road and reach the open country beyond.

A long time they waited, or so it seemed, and then suddenly there was a new sound in the air; the sound of men singing. It came from the westward, so faint and elusive at first, Stan thought he was imagining it. But instead of dying it was growing stronger, louder and clearer and soon he recognized the tune. It was "Waltzing Matilda," the marching song of the Aussies, and as he picked up the words he saw them coming towards him in the dusk. They were marching in single file on the side of the road clear of the main column and traveling almost twice as fast. Their faces were unshaven and haggard with weariness, their uniforms ragged and white with dust but as they slogged along, they looked indomitable and indestructible.

The file was marching in small sections with a short gap between each and abreast of Stan, the leader of the second group, who was limping badly, dropped out.

"Flipping boots!" he said, holding up the left one from which the sole was flapping loose. "They've just about had it. Got a bit of string on you, mate?"

Stan fished a length of marline out of his pocket and passed it over. "What's the word?" he asked.

"It don't look too good back there." The soldier sucked in his cheeks and spat in the dust, then squatted and began to bind his broken boot together. "The line along the Mournies Stream is gone. That's where we've come from...."

Speaking with a deep gravelly voice in short, jerky sentences he went on to tell what he knew. The line, it seemed, now ran through the olive groves about a mile west of Suda. Here the 19th Australian Brigade was dug in along a sunken road known as 42nd Street and his lot had disengaged and withdrawn through them. The Aussies hoped to hold there through the night. Meanwhile, this band of battered warriors, many of whom had fought all the way from Maleme, were making the best time possible to new positions in the neighborhood of Stilos. These had already been prepared by the Marine Commandos landed the previous night and they would be held until the last of the retreat, including the Aussies from 42nd Street, were through them and into the mountains on the way to Askifou. There would be another stand north of the Saucer and then the last one of all at Vitsilokoumos.

"Today's the 27th, ain't it?" the soldier concluded. "Well, they say it'll take three nights to lift what's left of us off the beach at Sphakia; and I reckon they won't start for another forty-eight hours yet——"

"Why not?" interrupted the Skipper.

"Because it'll take the main body all that time to get there; and that means we've got to soldier on and hold the approaches somehow for four more days and five more nights. What a flipping turn-up!" The soldier got up and stamped his foot to test his repair; then he slung his rifle on to his shoulder. "Hope it lasts me to Stilos. That road's a bit rough for bare feet. Thanks for the string. See you in Alex, maybe!" He stepped back into the marching line. They saw him lift his hand in a gesture of farewell and heard his deep voice picking up the chorus of the song: "...you come a'waltzing Matilda with me..." Then the gathering darkness swallowed him up.

"We'd better get moving too," said the Skipper, and a moment later, seeing the break in the column they were waiting for, he led the way swiftly across the road and off it towards the hills. When they were clear he looked back and shook his head. "I'm not sorry to be out of that," he said harshly. "It accuses me somehow; gives me a powerful urge to grab off a rifle and head west again."

"Me too!" muttered Stan.

"Well, forget it, son. It would be neither noble nor useful but just a stupid way of dodging a long walk by getting yourself killed before it starts. Come on!"

As luck happened, they struck a track almost immediately. It wasn't exactly a motorway but the surface was reasonably free of boulders and ruts and it led due south, climbing easily as it went. The night had shut down on them by now but it was clear and starry and picking their way wasn't all that difficult. They were both in pretty good shape and pressed on steadily while the going allowed it. So when the Skipper called for a five-minute halt at the end of the first hour, they were already well up above the coastal plain. Looking back they saw the glow from burning Canea lighting the sky. The battle had flared up again and the stitching of machine guns was added to the crackle of rifle fire; but it had all become remote, far-off, like something that had happened to them a long time ago. Up in the lonely hills, there was stillness and the night had brought to them a strange feeling of brooding peace. Stan felt it strongly. It seemed to him that what men did down in the plain didn't concern these age-old rocky ridges.

They had seen this same madness come on men before and were waiting now for it to pass as it always did.

When the break was over they pushed on again and now the country was becoming perceptibly wilder and more broken. The road, seeking the easiest way, began to twist and turn, sometimes almost doubling back on itself as it wound round great buttresses or plunged in and out of hollows and sudden ravines. But it was still making height and still taking them south. This they could tell by the stars and they slogged away at it, walking mostly in a silence which seemed to grow deeper as the noise of the battle receded. They met no one and except for the road saw no sign of human activity.

"Looks like we've touched lucky, sir," said Stan as they paused for another rest. "Maybe this will take us all the way."

"Don't kid yourself!" grunted the Skipper, looking at his watch. "There must be something at the end of this road but whatever else it might be, you can bet your life it isn't Sphakia. That would be too easy. Three hours we've been walking now and I reckon we're no more than six miles from the coast, if that."

"Six from thirty-five leaves twenty-nine to go!"

"As the crow flies but we aren't crows and there's still the mountain to climb. Come on!"

On they went again and a few minutes later the road dropped into a shallow valley. It crossed a stream in the bottom, and then climbing diagonally, ended abruptly in a T-junction with another track running more or less east and west below the next ridge.

"Now you see what I mean!" The Skipper pushed back his cap and scratched his head. "West's no good at all to us so we're left with two possibilities. We can follow this track eastward until we find another one going off it to the south; or we can forget there ever was such a thing as a road and make a course across country by the stars. What do you think?"

Stan hesitated. Sphakia was the objective and he felt an instinctive urge to keep on a beeline towards it. But the Skipper was getting on in years and though he had neither complained nor dragged his feet, Stan knew from the way he was breathing that he found the going hard. It would be very much more so if they left the track and it seemed plain common sense to pick the easiest way even if it took longer to get there by it. "Let's try the track for a while anyhow," he said, making up his mind. "The longest way round can be the shortest way home and we can't go very far wrong."

So they turned left and headed east; but instead of crossing the ridge as they half hoped it would, the new road kept on along the side of the valley. At first the slope was covered with low scrub but this soon gave way to olive groves and then patches of cultivation.

"Now we know," said the Skipper as rough stone walls suddenly appeared on either side of the track. "We're heading for a farm of some sort and it can't be far off. There might still be somebody there who'll give us a line to follow."

Stan grunted, then stopped in mid-stride, grabbed the Skipper's arm and stood with his head up, listening.

"What's the matter?" demanded the Old Man.

"I thought I heard something."

"What sort of something? Cattle? Sheep? A dog?"

"No. Nothing like that. It's crazy in such a place, I know, but it sounded like a motor-bike."

"Can't be. Listen again. Your ears are sharper than mine."

Stan listened and as he stood there, he realized that what lay over the lonely hills was not silence at all, but a stillness holding in it many sounds. Some of them were instantly recognizable: the soughing of the slight breeze in the olive trees; the oddly unreal sound of the stream in the bottom of the valley pretending to be a mountain torrent and fainter now over the intervening ridge; the nagging, nattering noise of firing on the coast road where the lost legion still held up the enemy pursuit. There were other lesser, nearer sounds, unidentifiable yet associated for sure with birds and small night-prowling mammals; but nothing that might have been man-made.

"You must have imagined it," said the Skipper at last. "The Jerries have the only motor-bikes left mobile on Crete and they're still blasting away at the remains of Suda."

He led the way forward again and Stan fell into step beside him. But he went uneasily now with frequent backward glances and a nervous tension building up in him minute by minute. Hitherto the hills, in spite of their roughness, had seemed like a refuge, a good place to be in. The Old Man had warned him that crossing them would be no picnic and he was ready to make any sort of exertion they might demand, to meet any degree of hardship on the way; but the only positive danger he could foresee was from the Messerschmitts, which didn't operate after dark. So on the face of it, once they were clear of the battle area all that remained was to make the fastest time possible to Sphakia. He told himself this now over and over again but found no comfort in it. Somehow in the last few minutes the covering night had ceased to be a friendly thing. It was full of nameless menace and in spite of all he had been through in the last two or three weeks, he walked like a kid scared of the dark.

The road was slanting downhill again now and after about another quarter of a mile, they saw the loom of the farm ahead. It looked enormous and the main building lay right across their path; a high blank wall with roof-timbers sticking out like a line of tusks along its upper edge; no doors or windows and no glimmer of light or other sign of occupation; only a gateless arch into which the road disappeared.

"Built in a square round the muck heap, I suppose," grunted the Skipper. "All the windows and doors looking inwards."

Stan followed him into the tunnel-like entrance and a few seconds later came out into the open again to find himself in a big courtyard. In the light streaming across it from windows and an open doorway on the right, he saw a motorcycle combination; then he realized the place was stiff with men. They wore the gray-green uniform and scuttle-shaped helmets of the invader and were closing in on himself and the Skipper with tommy-guns at the ready.

"Why they're Jerries!" he spluttered and turned with some wild idea of making a run for it; but the Skipper grabbed and held him.

"Easy, son. Take it easy!" he said. "A dead hero's no good to anybody, least of all to himself. Stick your hands up and keep your yap shut. I'll do the talking."

And with that they were seized and roughly hustled towards the lighted doorway.

CHAPTER 3

THE shock of finding himself a prisoner was so powerful that for a moment or two Stan's mind seemed to go numb and by the time he had gathered his wits and got it functioning again, they were in a big low-ceilinged room with an earth floor. A hissing pressure-lamp hanging from a beam shed a hard white light on a deal table across which an officer was staring at them dispassionately. He was a tall man, with a long face, hollow-cheeked and gray. His uniform was immaculate, his boots highly polished, his hands newly manicured and he looked as if he was freshly got up for a ceremonial parade instead of being in the middle of fighting a gory battle. Then there was something odd about his eyes, in one of which he wore a monocle. They were practically colorless and reflected no light. His face looked as if it had forgotten how to smile, or maybe it had never known.

"Please state your name, rank and unit," he snapped in English.

"John Gibbons, master mariner and Stanley Bryant,

apprentice, of the British motor vessel *Kyle*," answered the Skipper.

"Seamen! Then what are you doing here in the mountains?"

"I should have thought that was obvious. My ship is at the bottom of Suda Bay with the rest of her crew and we're trying to get out of the way of the fighting. We're non-combatants."

"There is no such thing in this war." The frozen face didn't alter its expression or the harsh, grating voice its pitch, and the opaque eyes continued to stare at them without blinking. "Continue."

"That's all there is to it." The Skipper shrugged and spread his hands. "We hoped to strike the coast road again this side of Retimo and then go on to Heraklion."

"And there?"

"Find a ship to take us back to Alexandria, I guess."

"So!" The officer considered them a moment in silence, then in the same flat voice went on: "Well, as our American cousins would say, it seems you have another guess coming."

And that was the end of the interrogation. He barked out an order to the guard in German, and a prod in the back from a tommy-gun started them towards the door. When they reached it Stan glanced back over his shoulder and saw the officer bent stiffly over the table absorbed in the study of a map which their entrance had evidently interrupted. Already it seemed he had forgotten their existence; either that or he had dismissed them from his mind as being utterly unimportant.

Stan found this a bitter pill to swallow, and the fact that it was exactly what the Skipper had tried to put across made it no sweeter. He wasn't used to being pushed around and he resented the suggestion that he didn't count. Then on top of this, he was furious with himself for walking so tamely into the bag; especially when his ears, picking up the sound of the motor-bike, had given him clear warning. He had relied on the Skipper, leaving him to make the decisions, never questioning them and forgetting completely that the Old Man was out of his element here, that his own judgment might be as sound or even, making allowance for age and experience, sounder. It would have been so easy to avoid the farm buildings and if he had trusted his ear and instincts they would have done so and still been free. Instead, here they were; in the very trap they had set out to escape.

But there was no percentage in bellyaching. He realized that; and he didn't blame the Skipper. The thing was to get loose again, and as they came out into the yard, he was alert for anything that might help him to do so. More than that, the simple almost instinctive desire to avoid capture which had brought him into the hills, had hardened inside him into an inflexible resolve to be free, whatever the cost.

There wasn't much to see; six or eight Jerries standing about doing nothing, another, obviously a sentry, marching to and fro across the door of a big barn or stable opposite, and the motorcycle combination, with three up, just roaring off westward through the arch.

The guard, marching them across to the barn, spoke to the sentry, who tucked his gun under his arm and opened the door which Stan noted was secured with a massive timber locking-bar set in slots on either side of the frame. Another quite unnecessary violent push in the back and they went stumbling across the threshold to finish on their hands and knees in a heap of moldy hay.

This was too much for Stan in his present frame of mind. Driven by an understandable but quite crazy urge to clobber the Jerry who had pushed him, he bounced back onto his feet like a bale of live rubber and whirled towards the door; but before he could start anything, a hand reached out of the shadows and, grabbing the slack of his pants, hauled him down into the hay and held him there.

"Whoa now, cock!" said a mocking voice as the door swung shut and the bar dropped home, leaving the barn in black darkness. "Do you think you're a flipping tank or are you just tired of living! Now do you sit still or do I have to stoush you? Take your pick."

"Okay, okay! But let go my trousers or you'll have the seat out of them!" Stan stopped struggling and the powerful grip on him was relaxed. "Who are you, anyhow?"

"Mitchell's the name, but you can call me Roo," the voice answered. "I'm from Queensland, north of Brisbane. Now there's a country for you!"

Without this information, Stan had already guessed from the twanging nasal accent with cockney undertones that the man who had just saved him from a foolish death was an Australian; and now before he could get properly launched on a eulogy of his homeland, the Skipper interrupted:

"How did you get here?"

"That's easy," said Roo. "There's two of us. My mate's up on the roof-beams at the other end working on the tiles. We walked here on our own flat feet. . . ."

He went on to explain that he and his companion, who it turned out was a sergeant of Marines called Josling, had been cut off during the fighting west of Canea a couple of days before. They had tried to get round the German flank to rejoin their unit, but the whole countryside was lousy with gangs of Jerry paratroops and they had been driven farther and farther back into the hills. Then they had found the east-west track and thinking it a good bet, followed it and walked into the bag exactly as Stan and the Skipper had done.

"We reckon on breaking out and getting back to Canea before daylight," he concluded, "if Josser can get the tiles off, that is."

"But Canea's gone and Suda too!" said the Skipper, and realizing the Australian knew nothing about the retreat, he brought him up to date with the situation, at the same time explaining their own presence in the hills and describing their capture.

While the Old Man talked, the marine Josling, who it seemed was always referred to as Josser, joined them. He must have moved as silently as a ghost because though Stan sensed his presence he heard no sound from him, not even a rustle or the whisper of his breathing until he asked a question. It was an odd experience, feeling these two close, hearing their voices, knowing that his future and perhaps his survival was now involved with theirs, and yet not being able to visualize them, not having a clue about what they looked like or what manner of men they might be.

One thing, however, was certain about them; they were quick on the uptake and the Skipper didn't have to draw any diagrams for them which was just as well in the circumstances. They were right in the picture immediately.

"This alters things a bit," said Josser as the Skipper finished talking. "We'll have to head south up the mountain now when we get out."

"You mean *if* we get out," suggested Roo.

"Oh, we'll get out all right. I've got a couple of tiles off already."

All this time Stan had sat silent. The presence of the German force so far south of the battle area had puzzled him ever since he walked through the arch and found them closing in on him; and now suddenly he shot out the question to which his mind had already fitted the only possible answer.

"The Jerries," he said. "What do you think they're doing here?"

"Got bushed, I reckon," answered Roo. "I told you there's gangs of them straggling all over the foothills."

"Yes, but this lot didn't look like stragglers. Suppose they aren't; suppose they're organized and on their way some place with others behind them, where would they be heading?"

"I never was any good at guessing games; you tell us."

Stan told them in one word. "Stilos!"

"So what?" demanded Roo. "That's east of here and we're going south. We should worry!"

"That's just it. I think we ought to." Stan leaned forward in the darkness. "Don't you see what it means? The re-treat goes through Stilos and the plan is to hold Jerry there long enough for the main body to get away over the mountain. Suppose this mob is aiming to outflank the rearguard and get athwart the road south of Stilos——"

"He's right!" interrupted Josser quietly. "And if they do cut the road, that'll be the end except for the mopping up."

Both Roo and the Skipper saw it now; but to them it seemed there was nothing to be done about it, except to keep their fingers crossed and hope they could break out in time to reach Sphakia ahead of the Germans. Stan however thought differently. He remembered the battered column he had seen stumbling wearily eastward along the coast road a few hours before. They too longed passionately for freedom and he knew there would be no sweetness in his own if he bought it at the expense of theirs.

"We've got to do something!" he said. "We've got to go to Stilos and we've got to get there ahead of these Jerries——"

"Don't make me laugh!" said Roo. "They're motorized."

But Josser agreed with Stan and then the Skipper pointed out that whatever happened to the road east of the farm, it didn't go anywhere near Stilos or he would have noted it on the trip he made. This meant the Germans were going to find themselves in rough country again soon and going against its grain which would slow them up and give anybody traveling light the bulge. "I think the boy's right," he concluded. "It might just be possible to get through in time, but I'd better stay behind. I'm not as young as I was and I'd only be a drag on you."

"Oh no, sir!" protested Stan. "They might take it out on you when they find us gone."

"I'll have to chance that. This has got beyond any mere question of your life or mine. We don't count anymore as individuals; only as parts of something bigger than ourselves. Don't argue, son. I'm staying."

"He's right," put in Josser. He had been doing some heavy thinking and now he produced the words of wisdom. "This lot we ran into is a reconnaissance unit pushing out ahead of the main body. They're in no hurry and they aren't all that sure of themselves. There's some pretty tough gangs of guerrillas in the hills and they're taking no chances of being cut off. Okay?"

"Fair enough!" agreed Roo. "But where does it get us to?"

"I'm trying to work it out," answered Josser patiently. "As I see it, Jerry knows nothing yet about the Sphakia plan and he'll never guess at it in a million years. Just think! Twenty-five thousand men retreating across a perishing mountain to be snatched off a coast where there isn't even a beach to muster them on, never mind a port a ship can poke her nose into. It's too crazy. Jerry hasn't the kind of imagination that stretches so far."

"What's he doing in the foothills then?"

"That's easy. He's making a flanking movement like we said but it's got nothing to do with the retreat. He must have planned and started it long before the line caved in west of Canea, that is, before anybody had even begun to think of retreat."

"Yes, but why?"

"You should know the Jerry tactics by now! It's a circling movement he's making, aimed at getting astride the coast road this side of Retimo to prevent the defense of Canea and Suda Bay being reinforced from there or Heraklion. But it could still put paid to the Sphakia plan. You lot wait there while I make a reconnaissance."

They knew he was gone but they didn't hear him start and after a little while he was back again, still without a sound. He reported that the hole was ready and suggested they get weaving. Stan had one more try to persuade the Skipper to go with them; but the Old Man was adamant. He wished them luck and, holding hands, they started off with Josser in the lead.

The barn seemed immense in the darkness and it was crammed with innumerable unidentifiable objects with hooked corners and sharp edges which alternately plucked at Stan's clothes, barked his shins and bruised his thighs; but he maintained his contact with Roo and presently found himself scrambling up a crude ladder to crouch on a beam immediately beneath the hole Josser had made in the roof. Twice he saw the patch of star-strewn night sky blotted out as Josser and Roo wriggled through the gap; then it was his turn and with his heart in his throat he followed.

His nerves were strung taut and the strength seemed to have gone out of his legs. Any minute now, he thought, we'll be spotted, and he waited tensely for a hail of sub-machine-gun fire to sweep across the pitilessly exposed tiles. But the air was wonderfully sweet and clean after the musty atmosphere of the barn and he instinctively filled his lungs with great gulps of it. The deep breathing steadied him; then he felt Josser's hand on his shoulder and suddenly he had forgotten himself and become absorbed in the job they had set out to do.

He lay between the other two and could see the shape and size of them now; Roo a long bean-pole of a man and Josser short and thick-set; but it was still too dark to make out their faces, and there was no time for speculation about them. He looked down into the yard. The light still shone across it from the door and windows but the idlers had gone and it was deserted except presumably for the sentry guarding the barn.

"Looks like it might be a piece of cake!" whispered Roo but before they could make another move a truck came roaring down the track from the westward, rumbled through the arch and stopped in the middle of the yard. The driver got down first and stood at attention then came to the salute as an officer followed and stalked away into the farmhouse.

"Can you drive a truck?" whispered Josser in Stan's ear.

"I did nothing else for the last ten days at Suda Bay," he answered. "Why?"

"That's our getaway! But he's left the engine running, so we've got to be quick. You do the sentry, Roo, and I'll take care of the driver. Got it?"

"Fair enough!" whispered Roo.

"Right. Give me say fifteen seconds start then get going. I'm off."

He slid away, ghostlike as ever, and after what seemed more like fifteen years than fifteen seconds, Roo gave the signal to follow. Josser had picked the spot for his hole with considerable luck or it might have been foresight. The wall of the barn immediately below it was strengthened with a couple of big buttresses forming a recess which was used as a muck heap. It was into this soft, smelly bed that Stan dropped a mere two or three feet after hanging from the eaves for a fearful moment of unknowing.

Roo briefed him in a single word. "Wait!" he breathed and then he too was gone like a shadow.

Crouched in the dung heap, Stan waited and he didn't like it a bit, though it wasn't the stink that bothered him. At the time he didn't even notice that. Staring across the yard, he could just see the tail-end of the truck and it partly obscured his view of the open doorway beyond. His straining ears heard the purring of the engine and there were other noises too; little scuffling sounds and rustlings and a rhythmic thumping which he finally recognized as the beating of his own heart. And as the seconds dragged by he began to worry. Josser and Roo knew what they were up to all right, he told himself; but they weren't supermen. Suppose they muffed it; suppose the sentry was more alert than they reckoned; suppose the officer finished his business in the farmhouse and came out before they'd done their stuff or a file of Jerries suddenly came stamping in through the arch!

He had worked himself up into such a sweat he almost jumped out of his skin when a hand came out of the darkness and touched his shoulder. It was Roo with a tommygun under his arm and a hand grenade in each fist—an assortment of hardware which made it unnecessary for him to say his job was done. A moment later Stan heard the faint cry of a hoot owl.

"That's Josser," said Roo. "Now, straight for the truck and don't worry about us but get her rolling and then step on it. Scoot, kid! I'll be right behind you."

Drawing a deep breath and stooping low, Stan shot out of the dung heap and across the yard towards the truck. As he approached it, he saw the squat figure of Josser leaning across the hood with a submachine gun trained on the door of the farmhouse and out of the corner of his eye glimpsed the body of the driver laid out on the cobbles. Then he was in the seat behind the wheel and feeling for the controls. His right foot came down automatically on the accelerator pedal and his left one pushed out the clutch; then his hand located the gear lever, rammed it into what he hoped was first and, leaving it there, groped for the hand brake. He was trying desperately to do as Roo had said and concentrate on getting the truck moving but he didn't need his eyes for that and they seemed to be looking in a dozen different directions at once.

He saw Josser heave himself up on his belly across the hood and sensed he had jammed a foot behind the headlight housing to hold himself in position; then, as he threw off the brake and flexed his ankle muscles to open the throttle, Roo appeared alongside the cab. The sight of his tall gaunt figure reared up between him and the lights of the farmhouse was all Stan needed.

"A piece of cake, all right!" he whispered to himself jubilantly, reckoning it was all over but the shouting and that in another ten seconds they'd be out and away; but just as the engine started to rev up and before he could let in the clutch the officer whose transport they were commandeering, appeared in the doorway.

The Jerry was either very jumpy or else he was no slouch on the uptake and understood what was happening at a single glance. Anyhow he let out a yell and there was an immediate rush of feet inside the farmhouse.

Stan had the truck rolling a split second later and out of the corner of his eye he saw a mob of scurrying uniformed figures piling up behind the gesticulating officer; then Roo swung himself aboard and dropped into the seat beside him.

"Duck!" he said tersely and lobbed a hand grenade into the doorway, yelling as he let it go. "Here you are, Herr von Schickelgrubber; pick the bones out of that!"

There was a blinding flash, followed by a shattering explosion which lifted the heavy truck a foot in the air. It rocked violently and for a moment Stan, crouched low behind the wheel, thought it was going over. But he hung on and as she righted herself, he slid into second gear and pushed down the accelerator. The engine roared and she seemed literally to leap forward across the cobbled yard with Josser still on the hood manipulating his stolen submachine gun like a garden hose and spraying the front of the farmhouse with bullets. Still holding his breath, Stan saw the loom of the eastern arch and headed her into it. There wasn't much room to spare but he judged it nicely;

she came through it without touching, shot out into the open on the other side like a cork out of a bottle, and bumping and rattling like a bag of hammers, roared on in the direction of Stilos.

They had made it against all the odds and now time was the only enemy.

CHAPTER **4**

THERE is no denying that so far Stan and his two companions had been lucky. To start with, when captured they might easily have been shot out of hand to save the trouble of taking them to the cage and guarding them on the way; but for some reason they couldn't even guess at, the German unit commander had decided to hold them, and that was the first break. The second was when they were locked up in the dilapidated barn with the darkness to cover their movements instead of being held in the lighted farmhouse under constant surveillance; the third was the departure of the idling soldiers from the yard at the crucial moment; the fourth the arrival of the truck; the fifth that it didn't turn round but stood facing the way they wanted to go; and the sixth, which was perhaps the biggest break of them all, the fact that the driver was told to keep his engine running. They had been given all the breaks and now were in the clear and on their way.

That sort of luck doesn't last forever and Stan knew it; but for the first half mile he was so busy fighting to keep the heavy vehicle on the rough mountain road there was nothing left in him for worrying about other things.

The truck wanted some managing. It had a left-hand drive which indicated a continental origin, but it wasn't German; more likely one they had captured from the Greeks; and it had been flogged to death. There was more than a quarter-turn of play on the steering and the gears were so badly worn that when Stan got in to high he had to hold her there by bracing his foot against the lever. But he kept her rolling and presently the moon, pushing up above the ridge, shed a soft light over the valley. This didn't exactly make the going easier but it reduced a little the hair-raising uncertainty of it and allowed him to breathe that much more freely.

Meanwhile Josser, who by some gymnastic feat known only to himself had shifted from his precarious perch on the hood to a more orthodox one inside the body of the truck, was rooting about in back, and now he poked his head through the flap and dropped his gleanings on the seat between Stan and Roo.

"As good as a perishing gold mine for us!" he said and proceeded to itemize the spoil. There was a map in a leather sling case with a plastic cover; a powerful battery flashlight; a pair of binoculars in another sling case; a Luger automatic pistol; another Schmeisser submachine gun and half a dozen spare clips of ammunition for it.

"What, no food!" demanded Roo.

"I thought that belly of yours was just about due to start rumbling again!" answered Josser. "There's two of those paratroopers three-day ration packs. That should just about see us through for grub."

The two soldiers whacked out the loot between them,

Josser taking the map, flashlight and binoculars. The third Schmeisser was offered to Stan but he refused it.

"You're forgetting, I'm a non-combatant!" he said.

"You'd better forget it too!" advised Roo. "From now on any Jerry who gets you in his sights is going to pull the trigger first and look into your status afterwards. Your best bet is to beat him to it."

"But I wouldn't know how to use it!"

"All right, then," said Josser. "Take the Luger and if you've got to shoot, aim low because she'll throw up on you when you fire."

Stan took the pistol and stuck it in the waistband of his pants; then, while Josser studied the map in the light of the flashlight, he gave the whole of his attention to the truck again.

The road, having dropped into the floor of the valley and crossed the stream, was now running parallel with it, still in an easterly direction. It seemed all right, but just when the tension was easing off a little the luck began to run out on them; and once started, it went fast.

They were back into scrub country again and the surface of the road was deteriorating with every yard they covered. Stan noticed the effect of the rougher going on the truck immediately and he didn't much like the feel of it. She wasn't pulling nearly so well and the engine began to cough alarmingly as she jolted in and out of the deeper potholes. Then the moonlight, which they had welcomed so eagerly, became a mixed blessing, throwing deceptive black shadows across their path. He found himself making minor errors of judgment and instead of blinding on, eased back the throttle and increased his concentration in an effort to avoid the worst places.

He kept her going for maybe another mile, the valley

narrowing now and the slopes on either side becoming more like cliffs as they closed in; then a great rock-face lifted abruptly in their path and he stood on the foot brake just in time to stop from running slap into it.

At first he thought they had come to a dead end but as the shock of the sudden emergency passed he saw the original valley had come into another running more or less at right angles to it and the road forked right and left along its bottom.

"Which way?" he demanded.

"Left's no good," answered Josser, poking his head out of the cab to see the stars. "It runs northwest as near as I can tell. We'll go right and keep our fingers crossed."

Stan had to back up from the cliff a couple of yards to get the truck round, then he gave her the gun and they roared off again. But this time they didn't get very far. Less than a quarter of a mile beyond the fork the engine coughed without the help of a pothole and died.

"What's up, cobber?" asked Roo, speaking round a mouthful of chocolate he had roused out of a ration pack.

"Fuel!" Stan put on the hand brake and prepared to get down. "She's been missing for a while now. It might be a choked feed pipe but we'll check the tank first to make sure."

He took the light from Josser and while they piled out after him, located the fuel tank. One look told him all he needed to know. There was a ragged gash in it low down on the bottom curve and it was bone dry.

"Must have been a splinter off that grenade," said Josser, examining the damage with an expert eye. "I reckon we're lucky she didn't go up in smoke."

"Well, standing admiring it won't get us to Stilos," said

Stan impatiently. "We'd better plug the hole with something and fill up from the spare can."

"That would be a good idea if there was a spare can but there isn't. I've been right through her and either she didn't carry one or the driver's flogged it." Josser pushed back his tin hat and scratched his head. "Looks like we're dismounted for the rest of this operation and proceed from here on our own flat feet."

Roo took a dim view of the prospect and made no secret of the fact. In language more forceful than polite he gave his opinion of Jerries in general then started on the recently defunct driver in particular. His vocabulary was extensive and he enjoyed giving it an airing, but before he got fairly under way Stan grabbed him by the arm.

"Listen!" he hissed, jerking up his head. For the second time that night his quick ear had caught the sound of a motorcycle and this time he was ready to stick his toes in about it. But he didn't have to. Josser had already picked it up.

"That's a Jerry patrol and they're after us!" he said, looking round. The truck had conked close in under a rock face which was almost sheer but split by a defile so narrow and steep a climber would have called it a chimney. He pointed. "That's our road. Up and over. Let's go!"

Seizing the equipment they had acquired, they scrambled into the cleft then paused while Josser carefully selected the best route to follow. By this time the pursuit was getting dangerously close. Stan heard the bikes check at the junction of the two valleys then start up again, but they might have been a thousand miles away for all the urgency Josser showed.

"Come on, Josser!" said Roo. "You can come back and admire the scenery after we've won the flipping war!"

But Josser refused to be hurried. "There'll be no back-tracking for us once we begin climbing," he said. "And I don't fancy being stuck on a ledge halfway up with Jerry taking pot shots at us, so we've got to be sure."

Making up his mind at last, he led them on to a barely perceptible goat track which wound to the right round a huge buttress and brought them out onto a ledge about fifty feet above the moonlit floor of the valley just as the Germans came round the bend and sighted the truck.

"Down now!" whispered Josser, and flattening out on the rock they waited and watched.

There were two motorcycle combinations each with three up and, taking no chances, the Jerries were off the machines and in among the boulders by the side of the road before the roar of the engines had stopped echoing from the rocks. Then they started to rake the truck with fire from their submachine guns.

"I've got three of them on a plate!" whispered Roo, sliding his own Schmeisser forward; but Josser pushed down the muzzle before he could fire.

"Wait!" he grunted. "There's six and we want them all."

They waited and presently the patrol, having failed to draw any response from the truck which by now must have had more holes in it than a crate of colanders, closed in on it cautiously. No doubt their intention was to dump the corpses of the escaped prisoners and tool the vehicle back to the farmhouse which was apparently some sort of forward control-point. So far they had taken no chances but the surprise of finding the quarry gone made them forget their caution and they began to move together on

the near side. This was precisely what Josser had antici-
pated and he dug his elbow into the Australian's ribs.

"The grenade!" he breathed. "Hold it till I give the
word."

Roo got the idea and making a low hissing noise through
his teeth, unhitched the grenade from his belt and eased
himself into position. The Germans were bunched now and
arguing about the next step to be taken but they never
reached a decision. Stan missed Josser's signal and Roo's
movement was so swift he didn't see that either. He heard
the harsh, guttural voices lifting clearly to the ledge; then
there was a flash followed by a cracking explosion which
almost deafened him and seemed to go on reverberating
endlessly along the deep valley. Instinctively then he
raised himself to see what had happened, but before he
could take in more than a glimpse of the shattered truck,
Josser pulled him back from the edge.

"No sense in looking when you don't have to," he said.
"We got them all right, but it isn't pretty. War never is."

Roo had no such qualms and studied the scene with
interest. This didn't mean he was more bloodthirsty than
Josser or got any sort of kick out of killing; but he was
tougher in fiber and, being less imaginative, saw things
more simply. He resented the war because it had dragged
him away from his beloved Queensland but he didn't hate
the Germans—only the things they stood for; and he was
in no way embittered by all the months of grim fighting he
had done. For him the issue was simple and he tried to
keep it that way. The more Jerries he killed, the quicker
he would get back to his sundowning and that was all
there was to it.

"You're a flipping marvel!" he said to Josser. "All six of

them as easy as shelling peas! How did you know they'd bunch up like that?"

"That's the way with Jerries. They go by the book, and when they come up against anything that isn't in it, they're like sheep. Come on, we've still got a job to do."

He led them away from the ledge into the back of the chimney and after close on an hour of strenuous climbing they reached the crest of the ridge. Here they halted to rest and review the situation.

Josser laid it off for them and he reckoned it looked pretty good. Roo's grenade had completely eliminated the immediate pursuit and barring accidents they themselves were out of the wood; but it would also have a side effect that was ultimately more important. When the Germans discovered the remains of the truck and the missing patrol they would come to the conclusion that the hills were strongly held by troops or guerrillas or maybe both; and fearing an ambush or being cut off they would abandon any idea of a swift thrust through to Stilos and advance slowly, consolidating all the way. His guess was they'd stay put now till daylight anyhow.

"You mean we've gummed the works for them?" demanded Stan.

"Maybe yes; maybe no. It all depends on how long our fellows need to hold at Stilos. But the least we've done is to give them a few hours extra to play with, which means we don't have to break our necks trying to reach the place before dawn. If we make it by noon, positions to cover the flank can still be selected and manned before Jerry arrives."

As near as he could calculate from the map they were only some six miles west of the road now; but it was six miles of wild country, ribbed with high broken ridges through which deep valleys ran every way. Each step they made would need to be picked and a lot of it they would have to cover on all fours, hanging on by their hands as they felt with their feet for the next toe hold.

"What I'm getting at is this," he said. "It's no sort of country for night exercises and now we've got time in hand it might be a good idea to wait here till daybreak. It can't be much more than an hour off now and we could all do with a breather."

Neither Stan nor Roo could see any good reason for rejecting Josser's suggestion and, stretching themselves out in the lee of a big boulder, they prepared to make the most of the break. It had been a tense, tough night for all three of them and the final climb to the ridge had left them pretty well used up and leg-weary; but Roo and Josser were quite content with getting the weight off their feet. They seemed to have forgotten there was such a thing as sleep. Stan however was dead for want of it. Lying on his back looking up at the stars, he heard the Aussie begin another chapter of his wanderings in the bush. For maybe twenty seconds he listened to the dry twanging voice without taking in a word it said; then his eyes closed and the next thing he knew was Josser shaking him awake in the first light of the new day.

He sat up and stretched himself, then shivered for they were already a considerable height above the coastal plain and the morning air had a keen edge to it. Behind him the valley where they had left the truck was choked with mist. It was thinning along the rim, swirling in slow wreaths among the boulders and ragged outcropping ledges; but below that it reminded solid, white and still as a foam bath, and he caught his breath at the beauty and peace of it. Then he remembered what it hid and turned abruptly away, shivering again but this time not from the cold.

"How about brewing up before we start?" demanded Roo.

"Daren't risk a fire with Jerry so close on our tails," answered Josser. "And it's time we got cracking anyway. Let's go!"

So they started on the final stage of the journey to Stilos, and as the light grew about them, Stan got his first full view of his companions who had so far been only shadowy faceless figures to him—one tall and thin and the other short and thick.

Now, though both of them wore a four-day stubble of whiskers sprouting from a mask of sweat-caked dust and grime, he saw they had faces to match; Roo's as long as a horse's and Josser's round as the moon at the full. Even allowing for the dirt and the whiskers, neither of them could have been called handsome and in their present condition any policeman worth his salt would have run them in at sight just to be on the safe side.

The Australian was dark, the exposed skin on his high cheek-bones and forehead tanned by sun and wind to the color and consistency of an old saddle-flap. He had fine eyes, deep-set, wide-spaced and so far-looking they might have belonged to a seafaring man. His slightly bandy legs were long like the rest of him and he walked with a peculiar slouching gait.

On closer inspection Josser too had his points. Under the dirt he was ginger and freckled. Properly spruced up and clad in a respectable suit of civvies with a collar and tie round his massive neck and a bowler hat on his flaming head, he might have passed for a butcher, a blacksmith— or even an archdeacon so long as he kept his mouth shut.

But before the war jerked him into the Royal Marines he was in fact a farm laborer doing a bit of lucrative poaching on the side whenever the moon and the season served. It was in pursuit of this time-honored but wholly illegal occupation that he had developed his extraordinary ability to move like a cat in the dark. His eyes were more green than gray. Like Roo's they were far-looking but shrewd and calculating; wary eyes which saw more than he let on about and brooded somberly far back in their depths.

Looking more like a bear than a cat with his immensely broad sloping shoulders, long arms and short powerful legs, he led the way and set them a cracking pace.

Down they went into the floor of the next valley and by the time they had picked a path through the scrub that filled its bottom, the sun blazed down on them out of the cloudless sky and Stan was sweating freely. Then came another tough climb to the ridge beyond, followed by another valley and another ridge and so on throughout the long morning.

Apparently they had shaken off the German flying column but the Messerschmitts were out hunting immediately after sunup. Fortunately they were under cover in a bottom when the first one came over and Josser was able to give them a timely warning.

"It's movement they're looking for; any sort of movement," he said. "So if one comes over when we're on the rocks, don't dive for cover; just flatten out and freeze where you are."

It wanted some nerve to lie motionless on the naked ridge with an enemy plane roaring less than a hundred feet overhead; but they did it, and although five more of the German fighters flew over at intervals in the next few hours, they were not detected.

Apart from the Messerschmitts the only other sign of war was the noise of the fighting coming from somewhere ahead. Starting up at daybreak it came to them faintly at first, a mere rumbling like distant thunder heard only on the ridges; but as they drew nearer to Stilos it grew louder and more continuous until around about ten o'clock it reached a furious peak then tailed off abruptly to an occasional crackle of small-arms fire.

"What do you reckon that means?" demanded Roo.

"Don't know, but we'll soon find out," answered Josser. They were just beginning the climb out of another of the endless ravines and he pointed upwards to the rim. "If this map's any good and I'm reading it right Stilos lies below the next ridge after this one."

"Come on then, let's shake it up!" said Stan. "I've got a feeling something's happened."

They pressed on, going flat out; but in spite of their will to hurry, the nature of the country continued to dictate their speed and it was just on noon when they topped the final ridge and at last looked down on the shattered village of Stilos and the road to Sphakia running through it.

Josser unslung the binoculars but Stan could see clearly enough without them, and what he saw made his heart miss a beat. Stilos was as empty as Suda had been the previous day and like it, no doubt, deserted except for its ghosts.

CHAPTER 5

So the task Stan, Roo and Josser had imposed on themselves was accomplished. They had reached the road ahead of the enemy's outflanking column; but with nobody left to warn of its approach, there was no comfort in the fact nor satisfaction either; only a feeling of futility which left a taste in the mouth as bitter in its way as failure or final defeat. And crouched there between his two companions high on the ridge above Stilos, it seemed to Stan that everything was lost.

It was a lovely day, that 28th of May in 1941; the sky deep blue and cloudless with just enough wind blowing to temper the heat of the sun. The country too, for all its toughness and inhospitality, was beautiful; the arid hills, golden in the sunshine, patched with silvery gray scrub and dark olive groves and away to the northward a glimpse of the sea. Westward a spur of the foothills hid the ruins of Canea and Suda; but the black pall of smoke still hung in the sky above them and it made a savage mockery of all the brightness.

"Looks like our journey wasn't really necessary," said Josser, passing over the binoculars.

Stan grunted and focused the glasses on the road. It was choked with men, guns and transport from the outskirts of Stilos as far back as he could see which was all the way to Beritiana. They were Germans and at last he began to appreciate the scale of the effort the enemy was making to capture Crete. This was no flying column, no mere raiding force making a gamble; it was an army and fitted out regardless. He thought of the ragged, battle-weary men he had seen slogging along the coast road a few hours ago and asked himself what chance they had against a war machine so powerful and highly organized.

"There's hundreds of them," he said, giving the binoculars to Roo.

"Thousands, you mean." Josser screwed up his face and clawed at his flaming whiskers. "And a week ago they were only a handful of perishing paratroopers hanging on by their eyebrows. Makes you think!"

"It makes me wonder," Stan retorted. "What beats me is how it's grown, where they've come from, how they got here and what our fellows were doing to let them."

"Air power!" growled Josser. "Jerry controls the air, so he has the bulge and us the sticky end. That's the way it's been ever since it started; and it looks like going that way for a long time yet."

"But you believe it will change?"

"I know it will. Otherwise there wouldn't be much point in going on fighting, or living either if it comes to that." Josser took up the glasses again and studied the road, trying to deduce what had happened as a preliminary to deciding the next step. He noticed that although there was a lot of "to-ing and fro-ing" going on with dispatch riders and staff cars, the column itself was halted, and this gave him the clue.

As he saw it, the withdrawal from the coast road had been completed, probably by daybreak, and the heavy firing they had heard around ten o'clock had been a counterattack put in by the rearguard to cover their retreat to the next prepared positions south along the road. This sortie had obviously halted the enemy advance on the northern outskirts of Stilos and, thinking the village was still strongly held, he was waiting for the *Luftwaffe* to come along and soften it up for him.

"Any minute now," Josser concluded, turning his attention to the map, "that road is going to be distinctly unhealthy."

"Which means?" demanded Stan.

"It's us for the high spots again. We've only ourselves to think of now so I reckon we should keep to the hills till we've crossed the main ridge and then work down towards the road, aiming to strike it somewhere in the Askifou Saucer. With a bit of luck and keeping going, we'll make it before sunup tomorrow."

Although time had ceased to be the all-important factor there was no sense in hanging around waiting for something to bust loose, and they got under way again while the going was good.

The ridge they were on ran more or less north and south and seemed to provide a comparatively easy route up the mountain.

"We'll drop just below the crest so we're out of sight from the road and that should do us nicely," said Josser, taking the lead again.

But it seemed they had run right out of luck now and before they had got into their stride, the first wave of

Heinkels came roaring in from the northward and the bombardment of Stilos was on. The obvious thing now was to put the longest possible distance between themselves and the doomed village in the shortest possible time; but Josser knew too much about the German method to chance it. This wouldn't be a few planes coming over to drop bombs haphazard on a cluster of houses but wave after wave of them used as artillery to put down a barrage. They would unload to a carefully worked out pattern and the ridge because it commanded the road would be included in the target area. The only reasonably safe thing to do was to find a crack in the ground in which to hole up and sweat it out. There were no crevices deep and narrow enough in sight; but Josser, who always seemed to be thinking a couple of jumps ahead, had already spotted a ledge with a slight overhang just below the crest. It was on the eastern slope, overlooking the village, which was the wrong side for them; but there was no choice and flattening out they crawled towards it as the first sticks of bombs began to fall.

The ledge was only a matter of yards away but it seemed like miles. Twice on the way, Stan was showered with dust and small stones from nearby explosions but they made it safely and hugging the rock, settled down to a grandstand view of the systematic destruction of Stilos and its surroundings.

Secure in the knowledge that there was no opposition, the bombers came in low at about one a minute. Some worked backwards and forwards across the village, reducing house after house to rubble, while others plastered the outskirts and the slopes of the surrounding hills. Stan's experiences in Suda Bay had hardened him to bombardment from the air; but this was frightfulness on a scale beyond anything he had ever imagined. It lasted precisely an hour and left him half-deaf, dazed and shaken by its ferocity.

Josser, however, kept his wits about him and his eyes on the column of troops in the road. When he saw them preparing to move forward, he knew the Heinkel just coming in would be the last and as soon as its bombs had exploded, he led Roo and Stan sharply out of their hole and over the hump to the far side of the ridge.

"Now," he said, pointing to a faintly marked goat track, "there's our road and we'd better step on it!"

They set off again and for a while the going though steep was comparatively good, which was just as well because Stan didn't really know whether he was backing or filling. He was a bit gone at the knees and his feet didn't seem to belong to him any more while his head felt like a balloon on the point of taking off or bursting. Between them Roo and Josser kept him going and gradually the effect of the bombardment wore off; but it was getting on towards sundown before he had fully recovered and by that time they were high up on the mountain and in rough going again.

And now they ran into fresh trouble. The goat track which had looked so promising led into a bewildering complex of gullies and ravines, to end abruptly at the base of a fifty-foot-high rock-face that was almost sheer. It took the best part of an hour and all the nerve they could muster to get over this obstacle and having done so they found themselves on a wide expanse of naked rock out of which two ridges, running south and parallel to each other rose like gaunt ribs to form a deep valley. The bottom of it was filled with a dense growth of olive trees.

"That looks like a pretty good place for a breather," panted Josser, heading for the shade.

"How about a brew up while we're at it?" demanded Roo.

"Too many Messerschmitts about to risk a fire." Josser jerked up his head listening. "There's one coming over now. I can hear it. Get under cover quick, just in case."

Stiff-legged with weariness they ran for the mouth of the valley and as they dived in under the olive trees the plane zoomed across the eastern ridge then banked steeply and headed north.

"Off home for his tucker, I reckon," said Roo. "And I hope it chokes him or gives him the bellyache."

"He made up his mind very suddenly, don't you think?" Stan was watching the aircraft against the clear blue sky as he spoke and now he grabbed Josser by the arm. "Look! He's turning to come back!"

"That means he saw us after all. Better hole up boys and keep your perishing heads down!"

Once more they flattened out and a moment later the Messerschmitt came roaring in at treetop level with his machine guns stitching madly.

"Only three of us!" said Stan. "You wouldn't think it would be worth his while."

"If Jerry's nothing else, he's thorough," answered Josser. "For all he knows we might have been the tail end of a whole regiment disappearing into the trees and he's taking no chances about it. Look out! Here he comes again. . . ."

Up and down the narrow valley flew the plane, giving it all he had. His guns were partly loaded with tracer which quickly ignited the dry undergrowth and when at last he packed it in, the olive trees themselves were burning fiercely. But after eighteen months of war Roo and Josser had nothing to learn about the art of taking cover and though many of the German bullets came uncomfortably close, all three of them emerged from the ordeal unscathed. Nevertheless the attack had already cost them valuable time and was to delay them still further.

A pall of smoke from the blazing trees now lay across the two ridges and the bottom of the valley which had looked like an easy way forward was an impassable lake of fire. There was nothing else for it but to detour, and grim-faced they started climbing again.

Josser had hoped to cross the main ridge in daylight and then to keep on down the southern slopes until they found a suitable place for camping at a lower altitude; but when darkness closed in they were over seven thousand feet up and still climbing. There was snow lying in the hollows now and the night was bitterly cold. It was no place for kipping in the open without blankets and wearing only light subtropical kit; but all three of them were pretty well used up and there was no guarantee that the day ahead would be any less demanding than this one had been; so reluctantly he called a halt.

"There's one good thing," he said, casting about for a suitable camping place, "the perishing *Luftwaffe* is doing no night ops. Not so far anyhow. That means we can light a fire without being blasted to blazes."

Being a bit of an expert on night ops himself, the place he finally selected couldn't have been bettered; not on a bare mountain-top anyhow. It was in a little gully with one side undercut. The overhang which had kept it free of snow formed an excellent windbreak and the bottom was full of scrub for burning. While Roo got a fire going and brewed up, the other two gathered a stock of firewood and then they settled down to make the best of the situation.

It seemed incredible to Stan that this was only the second night on the mountain; that less than thirty hours had passed since he set out from Suda Bay with the Skipper to walk across country to Sphakia. How right the Old Man had been when he said it was no picnic they were planning! He wondered how he had made out since they left him and then got on to the ifs. If they had gone with the main column along the road instead of being clever and taking to the hills ... if they had avoided the trap at the farmhouse ... if they hadn't hared off on that wild-goose chase to Stilos ... if he had never met up with Josser and Roo ...

At this point he pulled himself up with a jerk for he knew that without these two, their experience and crazy inability to know when they were licked, he would never have got clear of the foothills.

The hot drink the Australian concocted out of the paratroop ration packs was a milky sort of soup tasting of nothing in particular. It generated a warm glow inside them but it didn't last and the night was tough for all three of them. Even the fire failed to come up to expectations for the scrub was so light it never made a heart and as time wore on the cold became more bitter and penetrating. Huddled together over the alternately flaring and dying flames, they sat it out, sleeping in cat naps and between whiles speculating about the day ahead and what it might hold.

Roo brewed up again just before dawn and they were under way in the first light of the new day, once more scrambling in and out of baffling gullies, over savage ridges and still climbing.

Stan was stiff with cold, chilled right into the marrow of his bones to start with, but as the sun rode higher into the clear blue sky, he loosened up and soon he was lathered with sweat. The rough going had taken its toll of their clothing by now and all three of them were ragged as well as dirty. Red-eyed, gaunt with weariness and footsore into the bargain, they looked forlorn and lost and yet somehow indomitable as they slogged on.

Over ground as cruelly chopped up as this, distance measured in miles meant nothing. Each ravine promised to be the last, every ridge the summit, but it was close on noon before that promise was fulfilled and they finally topped the crest to look down on the Askifou Saucer.

There it lay, an incredibly beautiful upland plain, hemmed in by the savage hills like an oasis in a nightmare desert; fields, some cool green and others golden yellow in the sun; groves of trees for shade and little white houses clustered here and there among them; and through it all, winding like a narrow white thread, the road to Sphakia. It came out of the hills to the north by one high narrow pass and climbed back into them again through another on the southern rim.

For the moment the rumbling roar of battle was only a memory. The sky was empty of German planes and there wasn't even the sound of a solitary rifle shot to disturb the stillness.

"Looks kind of peaceful like!" said Roo with a sigh. "Makes you wonder if all the other lot—the flipping war I mean—ain't just a bad dream we've all been having."

Josser grunted. He was studying the road through the binoculars and presently he passed them on to Stan without comment.

Stan put them up to his eyes and adjusted the focus then gasped in amazement. The whole plain was crawling with men.

At that distance, even with the aid of the powerful field glasses, it was impossible to make out any detail; but their agony was plain enough without it. He didn't have to see the haggard faces, the thirst-cracked lips and the bleeding, stumbling feet to know it. It was all there in the movement of the column and the memory of what he had himself endured filled in the gaps. Like ants they were, creeping in long wavering lines which straggled and broke and made again endlessly as they moved slowly southward. This was another view of the retreat and he liked it even less than what he had seen on the coast road by Suda. Swallowing a lump in his throat that seemed as big as a camel, he set his jaw and gave the binoculars to Roo.

The Aussie took one look then swore softly under his breath. "What do you make of it?" he demanded.

"Fair enough on the face of it," answered Josser. Although he could see no signs of them, he guessed the rearguard was dug in to hold the pass through the northern rim. The position was immensely strong and pretty well impregnable to frontal assault. "All else being equal it could be held till the cows come home."

"You mean we've got Jerry euchred?"

"All else being equal, I said; but it isn't. Our fellows have been fighting on the run for days. God only knows what they're using for grub and ammo now. That's one thing and the perishing *Luftwaffe* is another. I reckon that's what they're marking time for now."

He was right again and they didn't have long to wait for it this time. The words were hardly out of his mouth before the *Luftwaffe* came in; Heinkels and Stukas flying in formation with Messerschmitts weaving fancy patterns around and over them.

"Making a flipping field day of it!" said Roo, spitting in the dust.

Then the bombs began to fall and the stillness was

shattered by the explosions building up into a continuous crashing roar that echoed through the mountains while pillars of dust and smoke spouting up from the passes mushroomed and spread in a dirty red haze across the sun. Once more Stan and his companions went to earth and crouching in a crevice that matched a grave for narrowness and depth, they tried not to think what was happening to the long lines of men caught in the open Saucer by this hail of death and destruction.

Their own course of action was still to be decided and in the brief lulls that punctuated the bombardment, they reviewed the situation. It was anything but clear. The only positive information available was the sketchy outline of the plan for withdrawal and evacuation given to Stan by the soldier of the lost legion on the coast road. According to him the lift from the Sphakia beach was to be carried out over three successive nights beginning on that of the 29th.

"Which is today," said Josser.

"So it is," agreed Stan, counting up on his fingers. "That means the road's got to be held another forty-eight hours after tonight. Think there's any hope?"

"Not for the Saucer maybe, but there must be other defense positions south of it."

"That's right. I remember now. The soldier spoke of a last stand at a place called Vitsilokoumos."

"There you are then. As I see it the main danger is still a movement round the flank of the rearguard to cut the road behind him."

"Fair enough!" agreed Roo. "But what beats me is why he hasn't had a bash at it already. He must have known what was cooking after our fellows pulled back from Stilos up the mountain."

"Too dodgy for him, I suppose. Jerry's full of bounce when he's got the bulge, but he's got no stomach for a scrap on anything like equal terms. If he left the road he wouldn't be able to take his guns and tanks with him and even his perishing *Luftwaffe* isn't all that much use in rough country against men who know how to disperse and take cover. Thing is, where do we go from here?"

The first and most obvious answer was that they should work down into the Saucer and join up with the main stream of the withdrawal somewhere south of Askifou; but although the plain was in full view there was still a considerable stretch of savage country to cross before reaching the rim of it and no way of telling how long it would take. Moreover if the Germans did succeed in forcing the northern pass before nightfall—and for all his optimism Josser had to admit it was a possibility—the Saucer would become a pretty grim sort of trap. Roo thought a better plan would be to detour again and join the road between the southern edge of the plain and Vitsilokoumos. But Stan wasn't crazy about either proposition. He had already seen enough of the road to Sphakia to last him a lifetime and wanted no more of it. There was too much suffering on it, too much heartbreak and he was suddenly filled with a great longing for the sea. It might not always be kind but at least a fellow knew what to expect from it; and besides, it was where he belonged.

"Let's forget the road," he said earnestly, looking away to the southward. "Let's make a beeline for the coast and take our chance when we reach it."

CHAPTER 6

WHEN Stan put up his proposition he expected to find himself in a minority of one. The mountain had already tried them to the limit and Roo and Josser were soldiers. For them, he felt, the additional hazards of the road would be more than offset by the easier going; and besides that, their military training must make it seem all wrong for them to be adrift and on their own. He stiffened himself for an argument; but he was overlooking the true nature of his companions and it wasn't necessary. They were nomads, congenital wanderers and though they had schooled themselves for the duration of the war to take orders when somebody with authority was available to give them, the lone wolf role was more in their line.

"Suits me all right!" said Roo without hesitation.

"And me." Josser squinted up at the sky. "Here's the next wave coming in. We'll get moving as soon as the perishers have gone over."

They lay doggo through another storm of high explosive and machine-gun bullets, then began to work their way back into the broken country west of the road. The bombardment was now so closely concentrated on the Saucer that they were soon out of the target area and after a brief pause to eat they headed south once more.

From the map, Josser reckoned there was now something under ten miles between them and the sea.

"But," he added, "that's as the crow flies. Having no perishing wings it's likely to be nearer twenty for us."

How right he was soon became clear. The southern slope of the mountain proved to be considerably steeper than its northern face and more savagely eroded. There was the same bewildering complex of ridges, but the hollows between them were more like flat-bottomed gorges than valleys. Making a line across them was a slow and laborious process.

A gorge which started like a walk in the park then became a nightmare of loose scree and finished with a two-foot overhang, took them up out of the first hollow on to a ridge sharp as a knife edge. It seemed like the roof of the world and lying across it getting his wind back, Stan looked hopefully to the southward for the sea. But although the day was so fine, a faint haze blurred the horizon and all he got was a bird's eye view of the way ahead. In any other circumstances it would have taken his breath away again; but with time becoming increasingly important and the strain of the last two days beginning to catch up on him, it merely made his heart sink.

They slid down into the next valley squatting in a cloud of dust and taking an avalanche of small stones with them. The exercise did the seat of Stan's pants no good at all and less embarrassing but more important he also ripped the heel off one of his battered shoes, braking.

Still heading south they crossed the scrub-choked bottom and then on the far side found themselves confronted by a sheer cliff. It was here Josser had second thoughts.

"I suppose," he said, scratching the dusty stubble on his full moon of a face, "we'll find a way up it if we cast around. But what then?"

"Another flipping precipice, of course!" growled Roo.

"Exactly. And another after that—then another and another. I'm just wondering if we wouldn't make better time following the bottoms."

"But this one goes the wrong way for us!" objected Stan.

Josser agreed but pointed out that so long as they kept going downhill and working to the right, they were bound to reach the sea in the end because the mountain sloped that way. "We might have to cover three times the distance but the going will be easier and take all that much less out of us," he added.

Stan wasn't all that crazy about the idea. The mountain was beginning to get him down. In its difficulty and baffling complexity he sensed now a brooding enmity and had visions of being trapped and wandering in the labyrinth of gorges and ravines until the grub gave out and they dropped exhausted; but he had no argument to set against Josser's reasoning and they slogged on along the base of the cliff.

So far they had seen no sign of life since leaving the ridge above the Askifou Saucer. The *Luftwaffe* was apparently still concentrating its attention on the road to Sphakia and even the goats seemed to have deserted the area; but presently the gorge which had been leading almost due east along the contour, turned abruptly downhill; and from the great rock buttress that lifted out of the elbow a number of faintly marked tracks ran to converge a little way below it.

"There you are!" said Josser allowing himself to crow. "Short of sidewalks and street lamps what more do you want?"

But all this had taken time and the day was almost gone. Already the sun had dipped below the western rim and in the bottom boulders and patches of scrub were becoming misty shadows and melting mysteriously into each other. Anxious to make the most of what light remained, they pressed on.

With the track becoming more clearly defined and gradually widening as the valley floor descended, this stretch was the easiest they had met on the mountain and the line of it was dead on for them. They needed the break for Stan, with his damaged shoe beginning to disintegrate, was limping badly and even Roo, who was used to tramping long distances in rough country, admitted his feet were sore.

"Any minute now we'll be coming to a village," he said. "And I'm going to sit myself down by the well and soak my flipping feet in it."

"It's about time you washed them. They stink!" grunted Josser. "Only give us a chance to fill up the water-bottles first."

"But what about the inhabitants?" demanded Stan. "They might take a dim view of having their water supply polluted."

"There won't be any inhabitants. I bet they're all in the bush looking for stray Jerries."

Josser reckoned he had something there and warned them to keep a sharp lookout. "I've no fancy for being bumped off by a trigger-happy Greek, so if we're challenged don't argue. Drop the hardware and stick your hands up."

"And what if they shoot first?"

"That'll be too bad; but I don't think they will." Josser grinned. "I've seen some scruffy Jerries, but none as tattered and torn as you two are."

All this time the valley had been widening in the bottom though the sides of it remained as high and abrupt as ever. It sloped less steeply now too and as it began to curve to the eastward again, the scrub gave way to a grove of olive trees. Winding tortuously through these, the track finally emerged in a cultivated depression which was a small-scale replica of the Askifou Saucer—too small to be marked on the map.

Pausing on the edge of the olive grove, Stan and his companions studied the place carefully in the fast-fading glimmering light. It was more like an overgrown farmstead than a village for there was neither a church nor any other recognizable center to it; only the patchwork pattern of fields running up to the high rock walls on either side and a dozen or so white houses scattered widely among them. Beyond the last of the cultivation which was a field of ripening barley the towering sides of the basin swung in towards each other to form a natural gateway through which the meandering track ran on to the eastward. There were no animals in the fields and no sign of life—not even a stray dog—around any of the houses.

"What did I tell you! Empty as a ghost town," said Roo. "Might be a good place to camp for the night. What do you say, Josser?"

"I don't know." Josser was still examining the houses through the binoculars. "Ghost town's bang on. It's empty all right; too empty for my fancy. I've got a funny feeling about it."

"Me too!" said Stan, looking uneasily over his shoulder into the darkness under the olives.

"Well you can scratch it on the way! Come on, let's go!" Tucking his Schmeisser under his arm Roo started forward and after a moment of hesitation, the other two followed.

The Aussie made straight for the nearest of the houses which was also the biggest. It was a low rambling place which looked as if it had grown there out of the rock it stood on. Three time-worn steps led up to the entrance which was closed by a door of rough-hewn timber bleached silvery gray by sun and weather. He lifted the crude wooden latch and as the door swung inwards at his touch, hesitated on the threshold.

"Either way we've bought it now!" said Josser pushing past him. Then standing just inside he lifted his head and shouted. "Hallo there! Anybody home?"

His voice ringing hollow through the empty house brought no response and Stan who, without knowing it, had been holding his breath, let it go in a long sigh of relief.

"Looks like it's all ours," he said and forgetting their premonitions they walked in and looked around. There was just enough light left to show the outline of things, and Stan was immediately reminded powerfully of the farmhouse where he had left the Skipper. Here was the same kind of low ceiling and floor of beaten earth, the same sort of roughly made furniture and, opposite the entrance, the same huge fireplace with a flat hearth and a flue above it big enough to wheel a barrow through. He sighed then grinned. "Better than a hole in the ground, I suppose!"

"It'll do!" grunted Josser and when they had dumped their arms and equipment on the table, he and Stan took the weight off their feet while Roo set about getting a fire going.

There was a stack of logs at one side of the hearth and a pile of kindling at the other and being a bit of an expert he soon had a flame creeping up through a heap of the small stuff. Squatting on his heels, he whistled softly between his teeth as he watched it grow. Nobody could ever accuse him of being musical but Stan recognized the tune. It was the one he had heard on the coast road by Suda.

" 'Waltzing Matilda!' For Pete's sake, don't you Aussies know any other song?" he demanded, then his quick ear caught a slight sound behind him and swinging round he saw the shadowy recesses of the room filling with men. They were all armed and more were crowding in through the doorway; young men and old.

He recognized them instantly as guerrillas and for a moment he almost panicked; then, remembering Josser's warning, he stuck up his hands and got on to his feet. Roo and Josser did likewise and for one tense minute that seemed as long as a wet Sunday they stood there, nobody moving, nobody speaking but Roo still whistling softly as if he didn't know how to stop. Then the knot of men in the doorway parted and through them strode a girl with a Schmeisser under her arm.

She was tall and slim with ash-blonde hair swept back from her forehead to hang loose across her shoulders; and though she couldn't have been a day over seventeen years old, there was great authority in her bearing and a peculiar decisiveness about her movements. In the flickering firelight her face seemed oddly fixed and expressionless as she measured Stan and his companions with cold unblinking eyes. What she saw however seemed to satisfy her. She made a little gesture with her hand and as the menacing figures round the room relaxed, spoke in English with a strong American accent.

"That song! You are Australians, yes?"

"I am," answered Roo. "These mates of mine are pommies; English that is. And you?"

"I belong to Crete," she said proudly and, advancing into the room, laid her Schmeisser on the table then continued. "This is my grandfather's house. Until he comes he would want me to make you welcome. My name is Elena."

The Aussie, obviously unused to the company of females, acknowledged the information with a stiff little bow. "I'm Roo Mitchell," he said, "and these two sundowners are Sergeant Josling and Stan Bryant. We're heading for Sphakia."

The ice having been broken by these introductions, Elena rapped out a string of orders in her native language and the guerrillas disappeared as silently as they had come; all except one—a youngster about the girl's own age, who set about preparing a meal. While they waited for it, Stan filled out Roo's bald statement with the details of their journey and the background to it; then Elena told them something of her story.

Her people, it seemed, had lived in this high lost valley for hundreds of years and belonged to it every bit as much as it belonged to them. Some of each generation left it to work in Canea or Athens or even, as her own father had done, to cross the Atlantic seeking a fortune in the Americas. But this was never for keeps. Always they returned to live out their days in the island. She herself had spent most of her childhood in New York, which accounted for her English and its accent, but the pull of Crete had been too strong for her father. He had returned only a couple of months back to be killed with all his family except Elena in one of the first German air raids on Canea. The girl had crossed the mountain then, back to her birthplace and when the Germans invaded the island took to the hills with the menfolk of the valley under her grandfather.

There was only a dozen of them to start with and they had nothing except their bare hands; but, prowling the battle areas at night, they got arms from the bodies of dead paratroopers and with men from other remote valleys joining them every day had grown rapidly in numbers. There were now between fifty and sixty in the group, every one of them sworn to fight till death against the invader. They operated only by night, grouping as darkness fell and dispersing again before dawn to work in their fields through the day. Being extremely mobile and knowing intimately every ravine and goat track in the savage hills, they were able to harry the German lines of communication almost at will and disappear like shadows before any attack mounted against them.

It was all tremendously heroic and exciting but, watching Elena as she talked, Stan found himself in two minds about it. He admired her courage but the cold hatred in her appalled him. She had only one idea, one single purpose that blinded her to everything else. It was to kill as many Germans as possible before they killed her; and that in a girl so young seemed all wrong to him. What the war had done to the *Kyle* and his shipmates, what he had seen at Suda and along the road to Sphakia since was bad enough; it had made him resent the whole useless, ghastly business. But what it had done to Elena roused in him a bitter anger against those who had loosed it on the world. It rose up in his throat like bile.

She would have gone on filling in the details of her activities but at this point her grandfather arrived and from the moment he entered the room there was no mistaking who was boss. The almost arrogant air of command left her immediately and after introducing the wanderers, she withdrew into the shadows to hurry on the preparations for supper.

Yet there was nothing intimidating about the newcomer, unless it was his fierce dark eyes. He was a little old wisp of a man, his face, incredibly lined and weather-beaten, sporting a pair of bushy white eyebrows and a ferocious white moustache. He knew a little English and filled in the gaps with signs and gestures.

This time Josser took on the role of spokesman and while they ate, he put the old man in the picture.

Supper consisted of a thick stew of meat and vegetables with fresh bread and a dry, crumbling cheese of goat's milk to follow and there was cold spring water to drink. Being the first proper meal Stan and his companions had seen in a week, it went down well; and not knowing when the next one would come along they stuffed themselves to the ears, a process which the old man watched with great satisfaction. He was apparently weighing them up and doing some heavy thinking at the same time and when they had finished, he addressed them in his halting English.

"You are tired and your feet are sore," he said, putting his gnarled hands together on the table. "Tonight you shall rest here and start for the coast at dawn with a guide to show you the way."

"How long will it take to get there?" asked Stan.

"We count it a day's journey to Sphakia and back but

you will not travel as fast as my people and will do well to reach it by nightfall."

He went on to say that while they slept, he would send out a patrol towards the Sphakia road to gather the latest news of the retreat; then he wished them a formal good night, shaking hands solemnly with each in turn and left with Elena stalking a couple of paces behind him.

Alone again, the three made up the fire and bedded down around the hearth. The earth floor was a hard bed but after the bitter nights on the mountain the warmth of the fire and the very fact of having a roof overhead made up for that. With his belly full of good food and his mind easier about what lay ahead than it had been since leaving Suda Bay, Stan was so drowsy he could hardly keep his eyes open. He wanted to talk with Roo and Josser about Elena and her grandfather and the guerrillas but the moment he put his head down sleep lapped over him and he knew no more till morning.

It was Elena's forefinger jabbed with painful persistence into his ribs that woke him. She had made a pot of coffee, and while he gulped down his share, gave them the news gathered by the night patrol.

The information was scrappy but Josser sorted out the hard facts from the rumors and added them up to a more or less coherent picture. Apparently a section of the rear-guard had withdrawn under cover of darkness to prepare the final positions at Vitsilokoumos, leaving the main force to hold the pass north of the Askifou Saucer through the night. Meanwhile naval vessels arriving off Sphakia at midnight had begun to lift the troops off the beach; but in order to get beyond the reach of the *Luftwaffe* before day-break, they had to pack up and pull out again soon after

3 A.M., leaving roughly two-thirds of the retreating force still to be withdrawn.

"At that rate, two more nights will do it," said Roo. "Do you reckon the rearguard can hold another forty-eight hours?"

"Against frontal attacks, yes; if the ammo and the grub don't run out. That road's just one long string of strong defensive positions. Jerry's only hope is to outflank them. He muffed it at Stilos but it beats me why he hasn't tried it again since."

"Maybe the guerrillas have something to do with that," suggested Stan.

"I'll bet they have," agreed Josser. "But it's time we were on our way. There's no rush, but the sooner we get to Sphakia, the closer we'll be to the front of the queue."

At this point Elena announced she was to be the guide and when they had gathered up their arms and equipment she led them outside and along the winding road towards the deep gorge that formed the eastern gateway to the valley. On the edge of the barley field her grandfather, who was waiting there to accompany them to the boundary of his property, took command.

He brought them quickly through the waving corn into the mouth of the gorge then turned sharp right to the base of the precipice. There was no track that Stan could see but without a moment of hesitation the old man started up the rock face and the others followed, Elena bringing up the rear.

It was a tough climb. Only an expert mountaineer could have made it without guidance. To Stan, however, it was worth every bit of the effort because when they reached the top and looked to the south, there at last was the sea. Remote though it was and blurred with haze, the sight of it acted on him like a sudden glimpse of home and while his companions rested, he took the binoculars from Josser.

"Soon now!" he said to himself as he focused the glasses on the vast emptiness beyond the last visible ridge of the mountain. And there would be no more hunger and cold, no more sore feet, no more backing and filling and wondering what lay round the corner. He would be back where he belonged and everything would fall into shape again.

Drawing a deep breath that was almost a sigh of contentment he turned to look back over the way they had come. The ravines and gorges they had traversed were lost in the confusion of ridges but he thought he recognized the point from which they had looked down into the Askifou Saucer on the previous day. It seemed incredibly close and marveling at the distance a fellow could travel in this sort of country without getting anywhere, he was just about to turn away when he saw a little knot of men appear on the crest of an intervening ridge. They were followed by others marching in single file and he knew them instantly for Germans.

There was no doubt in Stan's mind about what they were up to. This could only be the long expected and inexplicably delayed second attempt to outflank the defense positions and cut the road to Sphakia. He knew it and knowing also that Josser and Roo would feel impelled to do something about it, he was tempted to keep his mouth shut. After all, whatever happened now on the road to Sphakia, the three of them were in the clear. With Elena to guide them, they would reach the coast by nightfall and be safely aboard ship on the way to Alexandria before morning.

"Why should we worry?" he asked himself, lowering the

glasses and turning to look at the sea again. "And anyhow there's nothing we can do. We'd only get ourselves killed for nothing."

Then once more he remembered the gaunt man with the broken boot on the coast road by Suda and that was enough. He swung round to Josser.

"Look!" he said, sticking the binoculars into his hand and pointing. "On the crest of the next ridge but one."

And his guess about Josser's reaction was bang on. The moon-faced sergeant was about ten seconds weighing up the situation but no time at all reaching a decision about it.

"Jerries! Half a perishing regiment of them!" he said. "Aiming to turn the flank I reckon just like that mob west of Stilos. We'll have go to back and try to hold them."

CHAPTER 7

THE decision to put off what Roo called their trip to the seaside was made quickly and without argument, but there was nothing easy or lighthearted about it. The freedom for which they had fought their way across the mountain was now in sight and going back meant turning away from it again, perhaps for keeps. And they had no illusions about what they would be letting themselves in for by doing it. They were neither supermen nor heroes but three ragged fugitives from a lost battle with the taste of defeat bitter in their throats; and backed only by the uncertain help of a handful of untrained guerrillas, they proposed to confront a force of anything up to three hundred highly trained and disciplined soldiers who had got the sweet smell of victory right up their noses. Roo looked at Stan and Elena for confirmation, then summed it up.

"I've heard of easier ways of committing suicide," he said. "But we're with you, Josser."

And with that they got down to planning.

There were two things in their favor: first the extreme difficulty of the country and second the fact that the guerrillas knew it so intimately. It was their home ground, their own midden; and where the Germans had to feel their way more or less blindly, they could move with sureness and speed. According to Elena's grandfather, the enemy, left unmolested, would reach the valley about noon; but a dozen or so resolute men on the intervening ridges could delay his arrival for some hours and might even hold him up till sundown. So the first thing was to send out a party with this objective and Elena left immediately to see about organizing and leading it.

"Now," said Josser when she had gone, "that brings us to the question of defense positions in the valley itself. They'd better be good because as I see it, we've got to hold him till nightfall on the 31st which is tomorrow."

"What bothers me," interrupted Stan scowling fiercely, "is the old fellow and his family. I can't help wondering what will happen to them after we've pulled out. For ourselves we don't know and that's okay because we've bought it; but for them, whatever happens they'll have to take the can back, if you see what I mean."

"I see what you mean all right!" Josser clawed savagely at the flaming stubble on his jaw and scowled back at Stan. "And I don't like it either. But that's the crazy thing about war. Winning or losing somebody's going to the wall all the time. There's twenty-five to thirty of us here and something like ten thousand on that road between Askifou and the sea. Which is it to be; them or us?"

And here the old man who so far had listened intently without saying a word, butted in. He was a bit worked up and his English came out more broken than ever but Stan got the gist of it all right. It was that he and his people knew the consequences of making a stand in the gorge. Their homes and crops would be destroyed and they themselves would have to abandon the pretense of being peaceful farmers and become fugitives in the hills. There until the war was over they would be hunted relentlessly and some of them would die; but they would die free, and the valley would be waiting to give peace and human dignity back to those who survived. If this was the price demanded for the escape of the ten thousand on the road to Sphakia, they were ready to pay it.

After that there was nothing more to be said and Josser got back to his defense plan which had already taken shape in his mind.

The strongest point was obviously the gorge at the eastern end. By building there a number of breastworks of loose stone, each one covered by at least two others, he reckoned it could be held indefinitely against any force attacking without artillery.

"And what about the flipping *Luftwaffe?*" demanded Roo.

"That's Jerry's trump card, I know," agreed Josser, "and I admit we've got no answer to it. But what's wrong with foxing him into playing it too late to matter?"

"How do you mean?"

"Well, he doesn't know about the perishing gorge yet; not even that it's there, does he? That's the first thing; and the second is that he's got his tail up all over the island. It's been a piece of cake for him ever since the line caved in west of Canea and you know what Jerry commanders are—arrogant bigheads kidding themselves they're supermen."

Roo scratched his head. "I still don't see——"

"Your brains must be addled!" growled Josser. "Look! If the bloke in command of this lot we're up against runs true to form, he won't call in the *Luftwaffe* to clear the road for him until he's tried everything else and seen it's well and truly blocked. Will he now?"

"I suppose he won't."

"You bet your sweet life he won't; to him that would be just another way of saying he wasn't up to his job. That's the joker in the pack and we've got to use it. Here's how. Whatever happens, he's got to come through that olive grove at the head of the valley just like we did, so to start with we dig in along its western fringe."

"But that's crazy!" protested Stan. "Surely it's best to make the stand at the strongest point, which is the gorge. It's only common sense."

"Common sense, exactly. That's what he'll expect and that's how we fox him. When he comes up against us in the olive grove, still knowing nothing about the gorge, he'll think that *is* the strongest point; and I reckon if we can keep the gorge up our sleeve till tomorrow, we're home and dried."

He went on to explain himself in detail. It was time they were fighting for; thirty-six to forty hours of it; and nothing else mattered. As he saw it, Elena and her mob would slow Jerry up so it would be just on sundown when he reached the olives. They would check him there with everything they had and by the time he realized he couldn't bust through, it would be too dark to mount an air attack on the wood, even if he wasn't too cocky to ask for it. But he wouldn't start worrying yet; nor would he try any night attack; not after a long day of forced marching through tough country. Instead it was a safe bet he would back up to rest his men for an all-out assault at dawn, and that would be the critical point not only for the fugitives and the guerrillas fighting with them, but also for the battle-weary column on the Sphakia road.

"That dawn attack has got to fail!" Josser concluded quietly.

"You're dead right about that," agreed Roo, "but when it does, won't he call in the *Luftwaffe* to blast the olive grove to blazes?"

"Exactly. But it will be noon before they can lay it on. By that time we'll be snug in the gorge and when he tumbles to what he's up against there, he'll have to ask for the *Luftwaffe* again."

"And again," put in Stan, "it will be too dark for them to operate, I suppose?"

"Bang on!" said Josser. "And as soon as midnight comes, he can have it."

Assuming Josser was guessing right about the German commander's reactions and taking it for granted that they could muster the necessary guns, everybody agreed the scheme would work; but it needed careful preparation and they hurried down the precipice and back to the old guerrilla's house to get on with it, pausing on the way only to mark out the final positions in the gorge.

The grim-faced, fierce-eyed mountain people, roused by a messenger from Elena, were already assembling in the valley. Josser divided them into three groups: one under Roo to be responsible for the preparations at the eastern end of the valley; another under Stan and Elena's grandfather, to muster all the available arms and ammunition; and the third led by himself to select and dig the defense positions along the edge of the olive grove.

The guerrillas had made good use of the short time they had been operating and Stan soon realized that whatever else was lacking it wouldn't be weapons. They had equipped themselves lavishly at the expense of the Germans. Every man had a Schmeisser and most of them a

Luger as well and there were enough spares hidden about the valley to arm them all again twice over. There was plenty of ammunition too and a good supply of hand grenades; but the old farmer's proudest possession turned out to be a two-inch mortar. It was hidden in a hayrick with a couple of boxes of bombs for it and under these was a case of anti-personnel mines.

This last item seemed so important that Stan, leaving his gang to carry on without him, raced up the valley with the news. Josser took it very quietly but the gleam in his eye showed how pleased he was.

"We'll set up the mortar here," he said. "You get a couple of men to hump it along while I work out the best position for it."

"And what about the mines?"

"Better leave them. They're dodgy things to handle. I'll see to them myself presently."

"But you're going to use them?"

"You bet I am!" answered Josser. "They could make all the difference; and I've got a scheme, only it wants working out."

There were plenty of other things to work out besides this; arrangements for food, water and ammunition, allocation of fire power, provision for the wounded, a code of signals, a precise pattern of withdrawal and so on. Nothing was left to chance though soon the crackle of small-arms fire came down the mountain to warn them that Elena and her mob had made contact with the enemy and time was running out for them.

Meanwhile Elena's message was spreading outwards like a ripple from a stone dropped in the center of a still pool and in response the guerrilla force grew slowly throughout the day. By the middle of the afternoon it numbered between fifty and sixty and stragglers from the remote upland farms were still drifting in. They were mostly men, some quite old but among them Stan saw fellows of his own age or even younger and at least three teenage girls.

And now, while his squad put the finishing touches on the defense positions in the olive grove, Josser got busy with the mines. He spent a long time working out where to plant them and longer still arranging the trip wire by which they would be detonated.

"You see," he explained to Stan, "this is something else up our sleeve and I don't want any clumsy clot touching them off too soon."

"Better get grandpa to tip off his boys about it then," suggested Stan.

This was done and when the whole plan of action had been explained, the force was divided into groups, each under a leader who broke down the responsibility of his section into specific tasks for every man in it. Then, concentrated under the olive trees, they waited.

For Stan that was the worst part of the whole affair— the waiting. His mind was empty now and into it rushed all the doubts and fears he had been too busy to bother about. They added up to one single question; would Josser's plan work or were they overlooking some vital factor that would wreck it? His own fate didn't come into it and there was nothing heroic or nobly self-sacrificing in that. He was committed to the defense of the valley and so far hadn't got round to thinking of himself, which was probably just as well. But he thought of Elena, and as the sound of the firing from the ridges came nearer, wondered anxiously how she was getting along.

As it happened she was doing fine, and when at last the

head of the German column, still harassed by her sharp-shooters, came in sight at the head of the valley, the sun had been set quite a while. It was already dark under the olives but the light still lingered along the rims and enough of it glimmered in the bottom to reveal the approaching enemy. For the first stage of Josser's plan, conditions couldn't have been better, and it was all over in a matter of minutes.

The Germans, advancing in open formation with all their attention concentrated on the ridges, had no suspicion of the olive grove. They probably saw it as a heaven-sent piece of cover from the firing that had nagged at them all day and, bunching a little as they came nearer, suddenly made a dash for it. This was what Josser was waiting for. Putting a couple of fingers in his mouth, he let go a piercing whistle which was instantly blotted out by the ear-splitting crack of fifty Schmeissers opening up simultaneously. Caught completely unawares, the Germans tried to take cover; but the positions of the guerrillas had been cleverly chosen to command all the significant boulders and crevices and Elena's mob took care of the rest from the ridges. There was no cover from the withering fire and after a single half-hearted attempt to rally, the enemy suddenly decided he had had enough for the moment and withdrew. He took his wounded with him but left his dead where they fell. In the gathering darkness Stan counted fourteen of them—crumpled gray-green shapes—strewn across the front of the wood. He was glad the night would soon hide them from view.

"I never thought it would be so easy," he said.

"They were tired and ready to call it a day anyhow," answered Josser. "But don't kid yourself. It won't be a pushover the next time. Thing is we've got to keep them on the jump now till morning."

With this in mind, he selected a dozen of the most active guerrillas and sent them out under Roo to maintain contact with the enemy. They were to keep to the crags above him and, as Roo put it, lob in the odd hand-grenade to disturb his dreams. If they could do a sentry or two as well, that would be a useful bonus; so besides a supply of grenades, each man took a Luger pistol but their sub-machine guns were left behind.

It was a long uneasy night for everybody. Stan got in some sleep but most of the time he lay awake thinking back over all that had happened since he left Suda Bay and wondering what the morning would bring. He had stopped fooling himself about being a non-combatant, realizing that whatever label he carried, he was in the war up to his neck now; but he didn't like it a bit and the very thought of the next day scared him rigid. By dawn, how-ever, he had got hold of himself and with all his personal fears concentrated into a fluttery, empty feeling in the bottom of his belly, was ready to play his part.

As Josser had predicted, the dawn attack was a very different proposition from the tentative feeler of the previ-ous evening. This time while one section of the Germans maintained a heavy fire on the ridges and compelled the guerrillas there to keep their heads down, the rest ad-vanced in two waves, the second giving covering fire to the first. Stan was in a slit trench on the right flank of the wood and to him it seemed as if the whole valley floor was crawling with Jerries, while the air above him was full of flying lead. Hearing the bullets whistling past and thud-ding into the tree trunks, he felt a powerful urge to cower in the bottom of his hole in the ground; but glancing to his left he saw Elena calmly blasting away with her Schmeisser and forced himself to do the same.

Taking advantage of every boulder and bush, the first wave of Germans came on in a succession of short rushes until they were about fifty yards from the edge of the wood; then they went to earth, keeping up a murderous fire to cover the advance of the second wave. They were much too close for comfort now. One more determined rush would bring them in among the olive trees and that, however bravely the guerrillas fought, would be the end of it. Surely now if ever was the time to pull something out of their sleeves.

"Why doesn't Josser do something about it?" muttered Stan; then with his heart in his throat he saw the expected rush begin. This time the Jerries didn't bother about cover and, trying to steady himself, he emptied his magazine into the thick of them; but the dodging, bobbing, weaving figures were a difficult target and though some of them fell, he never knew whether it was his or somebody else's bullets that dropped them. They were closing rapidly now, and forgetting everything but the need to stop them, he rammed another magazine into his gun. Then as he raised it and squinted along the barrel, he saw the earth heave under the pounding feet. Across the whole front of the wood it lifted like a great wave, then disintegrated into a high wall of spouting dust, smoke and debris, shot through and through with flame. He ducked and a split second later, the blasting roar of a multiple explosion rolled over him and shook the walls of the valley. Josser had touched off his land mines.

And that was the end of the dawn attack. Uncertain now of what they faced, the Germans broke and fled. A few, more courageous or fanatical than the rest, tried **to** dig in among the boulders; but when Roo started lobbing mortar bombs in among them, they also decided there was no future in it and withdrew after their fellows.

"It worked! It worked like a flipping charm!" said the Australian, slapping Josser on the back. "Pal, you're a wizard. With a brain like yours it's up among the top brass you should be!"

"I'll settle for a place on the last ship out of Sphakia!" growled Josser. Then he reminded them that this was only the beginning. "We've got to hold for at least another twelve hours. You can start hanging out the flags and pinning on the medals after that."

This sobered even the jubilant guerrillas, and wasting no more time, they got stuck into the preparations for the next phase of the battle.

CHAPTER 8

THE first task facing the defenders was to reckon up the cost of the action in the olive grove. Stan, although blooded now, was still a long way short of being battle-hardened, and opting out of the exercise, he got the account secondhand from Josser. It was no surprise to him to learn that the Germans had suffered heavy losses but he was amazed at the lightness of the casualties among the guerrillas—two killed and fifteen wounded. Some of the wounds were pretty grim to look at but none desperately serious. That was the tally and it was one more proof of the skill and foresight with which Josser had selected and prepared his defense positions.

When the wounded had been attended to, the dead guerrillas were buried under the olives; but the Germans, stripped of their arms and equipment, were left where they had fallen. It was too big a job to do the same for them even if the mountain people had been willing to pay them this respect.

The next move was for the enemy to make and the question was what would it be? Josser, trying to put himself into the Jerry commander's shoes, reckoned he had three possibilities to choose from. He could mount another frontal attack; he could try to by-pass the valley by climbing out of it on to one or other of the ridges; or he could yell for air support and sit tight till the *Luftwaffe* blasted the wood out of his path. The last course being the one that suited the defenders best, steps had to be taken immediately to discourage any ideas he might have about the other two. With this in mind, Josser divided his forces into three sections. The first, which included the wounded, he pulled back into the mouth of the gorge; the second, under himself, stayed put on the edge of the olives; and the third, hand-picked by Elena, he split into two groups with Roo in command of one and the girl leading the other. Their job was to keep the enemy in sight and nip in the bud any effort he might make to scale the precipitous walls of the valley; but otherwise to leave him undisturbed.

"Do you think he'll attack again?" asked Stan as they settled down to another spell of waiting under the olives.

"Can't say yet," answered Josser. "But if he does we've had it. It was only the mines that beat him the last time and I used the lot."

The vital thing now, he explained, was timing. He wanted everybody to be snug in the gorge when the aerial bombardment began; but the positions in the olive grove had to be held till the last minute against the possibility of another attack by the enemy ground forces. If he evacuated the wood too soon and such an attack was mounted, the valley would be overrun and the attention of the *Luftwaffe* switched to the gorge six hours earlier than he was bargaining for. That six hours could be vital to the retreating column on the road to Sphakia. On the other hand, the German planes when they came would sweep in without warning and if he held on too long his own force could be wiped out by the bombing before they reached the safety of the gorge.

"So you see," he concluded, "it's a bit dicey and you'd better keep your fingers crossed!"

The morning seemed endless. There was no firing from the ridges and at first Stan drew comfort from the fact. It argued that the enemy had fallen for their bluff and was sitting tight until the Heinkels softened up the opposition for him. But as the minutes dragged by, the silence holding the upper valley like a spell became increasingly menacing and he felt his nerves drawing more and more taut against it. Presently he found himself envying Roo and Elena their mission. At least they were up on the top and seeing something; they knew what was cooking; but he was all boxed in with unpredictable possibilities and nameless fears.

"This is getting me down!" he said, feeling impelled to break the intolerable silence. "I wish something would happen."

"Be easy, son!" Josser looked at him round-eyed and patted his shoulder with a hand like a small ham that had been boiled with the hair on, then rolled in the dust. "It's just what we wanted and, believe me, you'll get your bellyful of action soon enough."

Giving him a stiff-faced grin, Stan resumed his watch on the valley and the silence built up around them again. It was mid-morning now and with the sun long since lifted above the southern rim, the heat was building up too. Already the rock walls, the scattered boulders and the patches of low scrub were shimmering in it and the edge of the olive grove was like the door of an oven. The guerrillas didn't seem to mind the heat or the inaction, but lay around in the shade catching up on their sleep.

At ten forty-five, Josser looked at his watch. "Begins to look like he's bought it," he said. "We'll give it another half hour then pull back."

Stan grunted. He was looking at a patch of scrub about three hundred yards away. Like everything else between the towering walls of the valley, it appeared to be jigging in the throbbing air; but he had an idea there was something solid behind it. For about half a minute he watched it, narrowing his eyes against the glare, and then he caught the glint of the sun on something metallic. Certain now and knowing what to look for, he covered the area with a single sweeping glance and grabbed Josser by the arm.

"That scrub bang in the middle of the floor," he said. "Do you see something in it?"

Josser stared a moment with his big mouth open, then he got it.

"Not half, I don't! It's lousy with Jerries!" His mouth clamped shut like a sprung trap and wasting no time arguing or speculating, he prodded the guerrillas awake and waved them into their trenches with orders to open fire and give it everything they had. He waited till they started and, when the Germans opened up in reply, picked up the weapon which he had chosen for himself out of the old farmer's armory. It was a British Lee Enfield rifle and he preferred it to the Schmeissers because of its longer range and greater accuracy. Checking the magazine and the bolt action, he stuck four spare clips of cartridges into the pocket of his pants and slid away through the trees.

And now once more the valley was loud with the drumming of submachine-gun fire and the pinging, whining whistle of flying lead. Keeping his head down, Stan blasted away on his own account wondering where Josser had got to and what they would do without him if he was still adrift when the enemy charged.

But he needn't have worried. Josser knew what he was up to and presently, clear above the stitching, rattling racket of the automatics, came the single, cracking spang of the Lee Enfield. Simultaneously a German reared up out of the scrub and rolled over sideways and, glancing to his left, Stan saw the round-eyed sergeant sprawled on a ledge about twenty feet up the rock wall with the rifle cuddled under his cheek. Again the Lee Enfield spat and another German lurched into view only to drop in his tracks. Josser had them on toast and there was nothing they could do about it. Five times in all he fired, picking his targets; each shot was a bull's eye and that was enough. Without even attempting to locate Josser's position, the Germans broke off the engagement and as they withdrew, the silence and the nerve-racking stillness of waiting descended again on the olive grove.

"A sort of feeler to make sure we're still here," said Josser when he got back. "And now they know, or think they do. You made enough noise between you to scare the pants off them; and there was only about two dozen to start with."

"And you got five!"

"That was the Lee Enfield, not me. It's supposed to be obsolete. Fire power's the great thing these days. But for picking them off at long range there's still nothing to beat it." Josser looked at his watch and slung the rifle onto his shoulder. "Well, I think it's time we did our disappearing trick."

"What about Roo and Elena?"

"It's all in their brief. They'll hole up until the perishing *Luftwaffe*'s been and gone, then work back along the ridges to the top of the gorge, keeping abreast of the Jerries in case any of them fancy a bit of rock climbing."

So the move to the eastern end of the valley began. It was done in a very orderly fashion. Josser was taking no chances and kept a covering force holding the fringe of the olives till the very last minute. The mortar was buried in one of the trenches to be dug up again at some future date when the guerrillas were able to knock off another supply of bombs for it. All the rest of the equipment was humped down the valley.

It was just on noon when the transfer was completed and the timing of it couldn't have been better judged, because bang on the hour the first of the Heinkels came in.

The air assault followed the pattern now so familiar to Stan. First came the bombers with the heavy stuff and not content with saturating the olive grove, they pinpointed every house in the basin in turn and blasted it into a heap of rubble. The Messerschmitts followed, skimming the smoking treetops and covering the ground under them with a blanket of machine-gun bullets and tracer.

As always they were extremely thorough. Apparently their orders were to destroy the wood and destroy it they did. When the last of them, banking steeply at the end of his run, swung away northwards the head of the valley was belching flame and smoke and it was a safe bet nothing remained alive in the vicinity.

Stan was shaken by the ruthless efficiency of it but not Josser. "I thought we could rely on him to make a job of it," he said. "Don't you see? Going by the book, he's over-reached himself again. With that olive grove burning the way it is, it'll be two hours, maybe longer, before his infantry can get through it. And two hours could mean a lot to us."

He was right, except that it was nearer three hours than two and well on into the afternoon before the Germans emerged and began their advance across the basin.

In the interval another group of guerrillas—three men and two teenage boys—joined those in the gorge. They came in from the east and Josser, through Elena's grandfather, got what news they had of the situation on the road to Sphakia. Again the facts were all mixed up with rumors and speculation but it seemed that after heavy fighting throughout the previous day, the rearguard was firmly dug in at Vitsilokoumos and the enemy had not attacked during the night. Meanwhile another four to five thousand men had been lifted off the beach under cover of darkness. The figures were the least reliable of all the information but on the basis of what he knew for sure, Josser reckoned it would still take two more nights to complete the evacuation.

"Doesn't that mean we've got to hold the pass till tomorrow night?" asked Stan.

"No, not the way I see it, even if it was possible which it isn't." Josser spread out the map and stabbed at it with a forefinger the color and shape of an overripe banana. "There's the road. What we've had to do was to stop Jerry cutting it. Okay! That's what we have done. But now our fellows aren't strung out along it any more. They're all safe between the rearguard positions here at Vitsilokoumos and the sea; and you can bet your boots the flanks of those positions rest on the edge of the cliffs east and west of Sphakia. So now Jerry can have the perishing road and do what he likes with it."

"In that case what are we waiting for? I mean to say, why don't we pull out now while the going's good?"

Josser had already considered this idea and, scowling ferociously at the map, he gave his reasons for rejecting it. First, there was the time factor. With the final lift off the beach put back till the night of June 1st, there was now no fear of them missing the boat and they had all the time in the world. Second, there was their present situation. They were neither hard pressed nor hanging on by their eyebrows—not yet anyhow; they had a stone-ginger of a defense position; they had already knocked a lot of the bounce out of the German flying column and the guerrillas were crazy to have another go at it. Finally there was the beachhead at Sphakia. The German force stuck beyond the blazing olive grove numbered anything up to five hundred men and the longer they were kept out of the battle, the easier it was going to be to hold that vital strip of pebbles and the approaches to it.

"We've got those perishers foxed now good and proper and it would be a crying shame to turn it in without another bash," he concluded. "When we open up on him in the mouth of the gorge he won't have a clue about who or what or how many we are and he'll expect another lot of mines and mortar bombs on his dish; so it's my bet he won't chance his arm this time but pull back right away and howl for the Heinkels."

"I know, I know!" interrupted Stan. "And they won't get here till tomorrow morning. We worked all that out yesterday. Where's the difference?"

"There isn't any. Only in what we're doing it for and that it's going to be a lot easier than I let myself think at the beginning. We'll hold on till around midnight like we planned and then do our disappearing act and make the coast at dawn."

At this point one of the lookouts sighted the Germans and after a final check of weapons and ammunition, the defense positions were manned to receive them.

Josser was right about the lowered morale of the attackers. They were no longer so sure of themselves in spite of the plastering the *Luftwaffe* had given to the valley. Fanning out from the edge of the olives they advanced cautiously and approached each house in turn as if it had been a blockhouse bristling with machine guns instead of a pitiful heap of rubble. This was all to the good because it took time, and it was gone four o'clock when they passed the last of the ruins and began to converge on the gorge through the field of barley.

Lying prone behind his breastwork of stones, Stan moistened his dry lips with his tongue and squinted along the barrel of his Schmeisser. With every nerve in his body strung tight he was waiting for Josser's signal to open fire but still it didn't come. So far in fact not a shot had been fired and an eerie silence lay over the valley. On it he heard quite distinctly the rustle of the ripening corn as it swayed in the faint breeze. It was a sad little ghostly sound like the sigh of a ship's bow-wave on a still moonless night and it made him feel a sudden uprush of longing to be back where he belonged. Then a wave of fear swept over him. Any second now the air would be full of screaming lead and shrapnel from hand grenades and this time he might not be so lucky. Suppose he stopped one! Suppose he never did get back. . . .

Josser, lying alongside, felt him trembling and laid a hand on his shoulder. "Steady, son!" he whispered. "It's the waiting. You'll be okay when it starts, which is just about now!"

His whistle shrilled through the gorge and was instantly blotted out as the guerrillas opened fire.

They were all braced up and ready for a long and desperate last ditch stand, but it didn't happen that way. Instead, the sudden blast of firing from the narrow gorge shattered not only the silence but also what was left of the German morale. The advancing line checked and wavered; then as Elena and Roo on the rim of the rock walls lobbed over a shower of hand grenades, they melted away. A few tough characters went to ground in the barley but the rest withdrew in considerable disorder and when their officers had rallied them, proceeded to dig in among the ruins of the houses.

As Josser had predicted Stan's fears had left him when the action began but he still looked a bit pop-eyed and white about the gills. "Looks like it worked again," he said.

"Up to a point," agreed Josser. "But I don't like those perishers in the barley. They're too close for comfort and if anybody moves they'll have him for sure. Besides, it'll soon be dark and they could cover a sudden rush from there."

"Look, Josser!" Stan's eyes went back into their sockets and were suddenly eager. "That barley; will it burn?"

"Like tinder, I should say. There's been no rain for weeks."

"Right! Stand by to cover me. I'm going to smoke them out," Stan snapped, and before Josser could make a move to stop him, he was over the breastwork and running.

He had only about fifty yards of open ground to cross but the hidden Jerries opened up on him right away and it seemed more like fifty miles. The first half-dozen shots came very near but he kept on, swerving and swaying as he ran; then Josser got busy with the Lee Enfield and taking their cue from him, the guerrillas weighed in with their Schmeissers. Between them they forced the Germans to keep their heads down and finishing the fastest run of his life with a flying dive, Stan landed unhurt under the fringe of the barley.

That was the worst part over and striking a match he touched it to a stalk of the corn. It was dry and burned all right; but instead of the flame spreading and growing as it ran, it flared briefly and died in a little puff of smoke. Match after match he tried until he saw with dismay that he was down to the last three in the box and realizing he was getting nowhere pulled himself together and started to use his loaf. Crawling about on his belly and elbows, he collected all the dry grass in the vicinity and arranged it in little heaps just inside the edge of the barley. He took his time about it, spacing the heaps to get the maximum length between the first and last and linking them with more of the same material into a chain. Then starting at one end, he worked his way down the line, touching off each heap in turn. The wind, freshening now as the night approached, was just right and the scheme worked like a charm. Wreaths of smoke rose lazily from the piles of dry grass, then the flames shot up through them, joining together to become in a matter of seconds a sheet of fire which rose like a wall along the edge of the barley and went roaring through it. The Jerries, tough as they were, had no fancy for being cooked alive and fled before it reached them.

So the attack on the gorge ended as darkness fell and it was not renewed before midnight. What happened after that Stan and his companions never knew because they

pulled out then according to plan and, leaving the guerrillas to hide the surplus weapons and ammunition, headed
for the coast with Elena as their guide.

It was no walk in the park, that last lap of the journey
for the girl set them a cracking pace; but knowing where
they were going and the certainty of getting there made
all the difference. They talked very little on the way, need-
ing all the breath they had for climbing; but Stan was
still troubled about Elena and during one of the brief halts
suggested she should throw in with them and leave the
tormented island.

"We'll get you on to the ship somehow," he said, "and
when we reach Alex, if you can't find any of your own
people, there's always the Red Cross. They'll take care of
you and have useful work for you to do."

"You don't understand!" she answered. "My work is here
and I have to go on with it till the end."

The flat finality in her voice told him it was useless to
argue and they left it at that, but the thought of what lay
before her saddened the rest of the journey for him.

At dawn they saw the sea and soon after the girl led
them into a cluster of farm buildings. There was a gate at
the end of the yard and from it a well-marked track ran to
the edge of the cliffs.

"This is where I leave you; and that path," she said
pointing, "will take you down to the beach at Sphakia."

"Won't you change your mind and come with us?"
pleaded Stan and for a moment she seemed to hesitate;
then she tossed up her head.

"No. Only go quickly now, please!"

But before they could move, a hoarse, mocking voice
spoke at their backs. "I wouldn't bother," it said. "I've

just come up from Sphakia and believe me there ain't no future any more for anybody in that dump."

Stan swung round and there was the soldier he had last seen on the coast road by Suda, the man with the broken boot. He was more ragged and dirty than ever, gaunt as a skeleton and his feet were wrapped in burlap; but there was no mistaking the wry grin and the quiet, straight-looking eyes.

"How come, pal?" demanded Roo.

"The last ship left at three o'clock this morning and they ain't coming back. All organized resistance is ended and it's every man for himself now."

Aₜₜₑᵣ eighteen months of war at sea, Stan had become
used to frustration and the last few days had hardened him to shocks but even so the soldier's announcement
shook him rigid. Feeling the bottom had dropped out of
his belly and the whole world was collapsing and becoming meaningless, he stared at the man incredulously.

"But—but—!" he spluttered then swallowed hard and
tried again. "This is the 1st of June, isn't it!"

"That's right and Sunday into the bargain."

"Well then, you've got off the beam. The last lift out
should be tonight."

"That's right," said the soldier again. "But they had to
scrub it. Losing too many ships I reckon. Anyhow the top
brass was flown out yesterday. The bloke left with the can
has orders to surrender this morning."

There was nothing else for it, he explained, and the
marvel was that so many had got out. With the beach only
twenty yards wide and a hundred and fifty yards long
backed by a cliff five hundred feet high, assembling the
men for embarkation and marshaling them into the land-

ing craft must have been an outsize headache. His own
unit was scheduled for withdrawal on the night of the 31st
and had started according to plan; but by the time they
got through to the water's edge, the ships had gone.

"Most of the mob are still down there," he concluded,
"but I've got a thing about cages, particularly the Jerry
variety, so I decided to chance my arm. I regrouped into a
unit of one, and here I am heading for the high hills. But
I ain't snooty and if any of you has a better idea, I'll throw
in with you; only spill it quick because there ain't all that
much time."

Having said his piece, the soldier draped himself on the
gate and waited for the response. He looked done up. A
bullet or shell splinter had clipped the top off his right ear
and the blood from it was caked with the dirt and sweat in
the stubble on his jaw. On the other side the sleeve of his
battle-blouse was slit from wrist to shoulder and a blood-
stained bandage covered another wound on the naked arm
above the elbow. No self-respecting scarecrow would have
consorted with him, yet his indomitable spirit still showed
through and Stan felt powerfully drawn towards him.

"You're an Aussie, aren't you?" he asked curiously after
introducing his companions.

"No. I come from London. Outskirts of it that is. Barnet
way. Run a filling station and repair shop on the Great
North Road. Or I did before I got mixed up with this lark."

They got down to ways and means then and at first it
seemed that having rejected all thought of surrendering,
there was nothing else for it but to go back into the mountains with Elena and join the guerrillas. But Stan wouldn't
have it. He was in sight of the sea now, the smell of it was
strong in his nostrils and he wasn't turning his back on it
again. The possibility of reaching Sphakia too late had

haunted him all the way from Suda Bay and his mind was already made up about what to do if it happened.

"What's wrong with stealing a boat and getting out on our own?" he demanded.

"Have a heart, pal!" said Roo. "There's a whole lot wrong with it. To start off, suppose there ain't no flipping boat to steal?"

"All right, suppose there isn't! There'll be plenty of wreckage and empty drums about. We'll make a raft."

"And then?"

"We'll push off on it, of course, and sail across to the African coast. It's only about two hundred miles and with any luck we'd do it in a fortnight."

"If we try that caper, it won't be luck we need but a flipping miracle," growled Roo. He disliked the sea intensely. For one thing it made him sick; for another it wouldn't stay put; and although he didn't mind getting wet, he liked to be able to keep at least one foot on the bottom. "No. I reckon we should take to the hills and play cops and robbers with Jerry till he turns it in. How about you, Josser?"

"The war's going to last a long time yet," answered Josser. "I'm for having a bash at Stan's idea. What do you say, soldier?"

"Clitterhouse is the name, Enoch Clitterhouse; but don't let that bother you. I answer to Joe." The soldier sucked in his cheeks, spat across the gate into the dust and turned to Stan. "Know anything about boats?"

"They're my job; or part of it. I'm a Merchant Service apprentice."

"I see. That accounts for the look—in your eyes, I mean; half here, half somewhere else a long way off. I'm with you and the sergeant. It'll get the weight off my feet any-how. I'll appreciate that, believe me."

So it was three to one against Roo, but he wouldn't be persuaded and, acutely aware of time stealing away on them, they wasted no more of it arguing but said their good-byes and parted.

Looking round as he climbed the gate after Josser and Joe Clitterhouse, Stan saw the Aussie and Elena had already started back towards the towering mountain. They were singing as they went. For a moment or two the words of the song came clearly to him: ". . . you come a'waltzing Matilda with me . . ." then they turned a corner of the farm buildings and their voices died away.

Feeling like crying his eyes out, he hurried after his companions and fell into step beside them.

It was only a couple of minutes' brisk walk to the edge of the cliff, and looking over when they reached it, Stan felt his heart leap exultantly into his throat, for there, right beneath them and only about twenty yards offshore lay a deserted landing-craft. She was only an open steel lighter, flat-bottomed, and square at both ends, with a couple of engines bunged in aft to make her mobile and capable of maneuvering. The fore-end was hinged along the bottom so it could be dropped to form a landing brow or gangway and the after-end, lifting clear, curved inboard to make a protective canopy for the engines. It was stretch-ing things quite a bit to call such a crude and elementary contraption a boat at all, and she was battered and dilapi-dated into the bargain; but to Stan she was the most beau-tiful sight his eyes had beheld in all his short life.

"There she is!" he said. "Come on, let's go!"

"Hold it a minute, Stan!" Josser was examining the beach and cliff-face through the binoculars. "The whole place is crawling with our fellows. There must be something wrong with that old tin can or some of them would have grabbed it off and been out and away in it long since."

Stan looked then. A thin haze was moving in from seaward but it hadn't yet reached the land and the early morning light was pitilessly clear. In it he saw the beach was littered with abandoned equipment and stores and everywhere, as Josser had just said, there were exhausted, battle-weary men. Many of them lay sleeping where they had fallen among the junk; others were stumbling aimlessly about the shingle; and others again, anticipating the frightfulness to come, crouched on ledges and in hollows on the cliff or lay half-buried in holes they had scooped for themselves along its base. This was the debris of defeat and the sight of it sobered him like a bucket of iced water over his head would have done. His eyes went bleak and he caught his bottom lip between his teeth. Beside him, Joe was cursing under his breath; the swear words came out of him in a long string, like a list of groceries.

"It was easier in the dark!" he said, reaching the end of his vocabulary. "Lot of them wounded too. All of them hungry. Reckon we're lucky. What do you think, kid? About the barge I mean."

"Well, it's no good sitting here like three fried eggs," snapped Stan. "We could call it a day and head back after Roo and Elena. But it's not only us now. That lighter could be a way out for at least eighty of those fellows down there; maybe a hundred at a pinch; so whatever's wrong with her, we've got to put it right and give that many the option of coming with us."

Joe, staring at Stan with expressionless eyes, sucked in his hollow cheeks as if he was rolling the proposition on his tongue to get the flavor of it; then he looked at Josser and nodded his agreement.

"Okay!" said the sergeant. "Let's get weaving."

So over the edge they went; and knowing that any minute now would bring in the enemy for the mopping up, they threw all caution to the winds and came down the cliff-face like a trio of mountain goats.

It was a hair-raising descent but they made it safely and then divided forces. Josser's part was to find among the hundreds of men lying and sitting around on the beach, up to eighty who were fit enough and willing to stake their lives on the slim chance of freedom offered by the landing craft. When he had assembled his party, they were to scrounge among the junk and pick up anything that might be useful; food, fuel and containers for water in particular. Meanwhile Stan and Joe would swim off to the lighter, put right whatever was wrong with her then bring her inshore. They were to remember that time was everything and not bother about her general condition but concentrate on getting her under way.

Picking a careful path through the clusters of silent, dejected men, Stan came to the water's edge, stripped off to his underpants and plunged into the sea with Joe at his back. They were both strong swimmers and in a matter of seconds were alongside the derelict scow, making a quick preliminary examination.

The first thing they saw was that she had run up on a sand bank. This accounted for the fact that she hadn't drifted away when abandoned. Apparently she had suffered no damage in the grounding. Her bottom was foul because she had been in the water a long time, but otherwise she seemed sound enough. Coming round under the stern, however, they found the trouble. She had twin screws and a mooring wire had somehow become tangled up with both of them to immobilize the engines. They could see it quite plainly in the clear water.

"That's it," said Stan. "Thing is, how do we clear it?"

"Looks like a hammer and chisel job," grunted Joe.

"That would mean beaching her, and there isn't time even if we had the tools. Stand by while I have a closer look."

Taking a deep breath, Stan ducked under, and holding on to one of the screws, examined the ravel. He took his time about it and his lungs were almost bursting when he surfaced again.

"I think I've got it!" he gasped, shaking the water out of his eyes. "There's an eye on the end of the wire and it's caught on one of the blades of the starboard screw. From there it goes four times round the boss then bar tight across to the port screw which has seven turns wound on it the other way."

"Very interesting!" said Joe, flat-voiced and blank-faced. "And then?"

"Well, it's pretty easy to see what happened. I reckon she had been going astern on the starboard engine and whoever was working her gave the signal to stop. The engine was cut but just before the screw stopped turning, it picked up the wire by the eye. Then not knowing what had happened, he went ahead on the port engine. There must have been a kink farther along the wire and the port screw promptly fouled that, took up the slack between it and the eye and stopped the engines both dead. Get it?"

"I'll take your word for it; but where does it get us?"

"Africa with any luck! Don't you see all we've got to do is reverse the process, turning the engines by hand with the clutch in. Seven revolutions astern on the port then four ahead on the starboard."

Joe had it then and scrambling aboard manipulated the engines while Stan in the water eased the wire clear. It worked like a charm and there was no more difficulty. The gaunt-faced soldier knew engines inside out and in no time at all, once the propellers were clear, had those of the landing craft checked over and running.

Being flat-bottomed, she slid off the bank immediately the screws started pulling her astern and Stan, hardly daring to believe their luck yet, headed in and ran her up on the beach.

Josser was waiting, looking anxiously at his watch, the sky and the cliff top in turn. He had assembled a collection of scarecrows and a heap of stores and was sweating about the time.

"It's half past eight and Jerry must have finished his breakfast long since," he said. "Any minute now the balloon's going up. It must. But we've got all this lot to sort out and stow besides filling up the water. It'll take a couple of hours at least and we haven't got that sort of time left!"

Stan took the point and bent his mind on it as he scrambled into his clothes. It was all right for Josser to talk about time, but they were taking enough chances as it was without going off half-cocked, and a little preliminary organization might make the difference between success and the failure that would mean curtains for the lot of them. Scowling fiercely he stooped to do up his battered shoes, then suddenly jerked erect as if he had been kicked in the pants.

"I've got it, Josser!" he said, grabbing the map and pointing with his forefinger. "I've just remembered. There's

two small islands in the bay. Here they are, look! Gavdopula and Gavdhos. We'll just chuck everything aboard
any old how and head for Gavdopula. It's the smallest of
the two and least likely to be occupied; also it's less than
twenty miles off and we'll make it by noon. This haze is
still thick enough to hide us from the *Luftwaffe* till we get
clear and we can hole up there till we're watered and
properly organized. What say?"

Josser, perhaps grudging the time and breath it would
take to say anything at all, snapped his fingers instead and
got busy on the stores with his gang of ragamuffins.

Apart from a few curious characters who stood around
wisecracking, nobody took much notice of what was going
on; but at the last minute another dozen or so decided to
have a bash and scrambled aboard as the brow was raised.

It was nine o'clock when the lighter, piled high with
stores and crammed with men, pushed off and she got
away just in time. The Heinkels and Stukas were already
flying in from the north when Stan got her round and as
he headed her into the haze and the beach receded astern,
he heard the thud of bombs exploding on the cliff top.

"That's the start of it!" said Josser, looking back bleak-
eyed. "The communiqués will call it the systematic reduc-
tion of the defense positions and there won't be a blind
word about the poor perishers it kills and maims. That's
war, son! The longer it goes on the crazier it gets and the
less men's lives count in the reckoning. And in the end it's
still got to be talked out round a table."

"I know." Stan was remembering what he had seen
along the road to Sphakia and the thought of what was
happening now to the hundreds of half starved, ragged
men, left worn out and hopeless between Vitsilokoumos

and the sea tore at his guts. He swallowed hard and turned away to hide his eyes.

"Your generation," Josser went on, giving himself a party, "must hate the tripes of mine for letting this happen. But when we've seen it through, it'll be up to you; and if ever you let the perishing politicians start another, you'll deserve all you get."

He pushed off to supervise the safe stowage of the stores and with an effort Stan fixed his mind on the landing craft and the task of bringing her safely and quickly to Gavdopula.

There was only a slight northerly breeze and the sea was smooth but, clear of the land, a long, almost invisible swell was running. Meeting it, the flat-bottomed scow pitched ponderously and feeling her lift under his feet, he cheered up a bit. The movement told him he was back where he belonged and though he couldn't shake off the haunting memories, something seemed to come into him from the sea to overlay them. It was a feeling of elation, and it brought with it not only a return of confidence but a renewal of strength and vigor. For a moment he had the queer impression that he was twelve feet high and fit to push a bus over; then the sight of the men packed in the well of the lighter reminded him of the responsibility he carried and his limitations—all these lives in his hands and the knowledge and experience of less than two years' seafaring with which to preserve and bring them to safety. That cut him down to size and he got on with the job.

Riding high in the water on her flat bottom the landing craft was stable enough but slow on the helm. This didn't matter much just then but he couldn't help wondering what she'd be like if the sea got up.

"We'll just have to keep our fingers crossed and hope

the weather holds," he told himself and then started
worrying in case they missed the island in the haze which
seemed to be thickening instead of clearing. It would be
an easy thing to do. There was no compass aboard and
he had only a rough idea from Josser's map of the direction in which it lay. As near as he could judge by the
wake, she was doing about six knots and as eleven o'clock
drew near with nothing in sight he began to sweat.

"Do you fancy a bellyful of ulcers?" demanded Joe,
leaving the puttering engines for a minute to stand beside
him.

"Not much. Why?"

"That's all worrying gets you. Lay off it, kid. We've got
a long way to go."

"But I can't help worrying. We should have seen something by now!"

"So what? This is a blind chance we're on. There's no
schedule to it."

It was sound advice but easier given than acted on and
Stan was still trying to get hold of himself when just on the
hour the loom of Gavdopula was sighted and his immediate fears put to flight.

There was still the possibility that the Germans had
stuck a garrison on the island, however, and while they
ran in, looking for a suitable landing place, Josser called
for volunteers. Out of a large mob of the willing, he organized an assault unit of tough types and armed them to the
teeth, and by the time he had them ready Stan had found
what looked like the ideal spot.

It was a narrow strip of shelving beach at the base of a
deeply undercut cliff. The overhang would hide them
from any prowling aircraft and, right alongside, the bed

of a stream offered a reasonable though somewhat steep and rugged passage into the interior of the island.

Stan, who was getting the feel of the old scow now, beached her gently and as the brow was lowered, Josser and his heroes charged ashore and up the gully.

They met no opposition and presently returned with the news that the island was deserted.

"So far, so good!" said Stan and, feeling the worst part of their struggle was now behind them, they got down to the careful preparation and planning of the next and final phase.

CHAPTER **10**

To the ragged remnant of the garrison of Crete which Stan and his two companions had snatched off the beach at Sphakia, Gavdopula wasn't far short of paradise. Since the first air-borne assault on Maleme they had endured ten days of forced marching and savage fighting under constant attack from the air. Handicapped by the fearful confusion and disorganization of defeat, outnumbered and out-gunned, short of food and ammunition and totally unable to hit back in any way at the rampant *Luftwaffe,* they had contested fiercely every yard of the long road from Canea through Stilos and Askifou to the sea. By doing so they had helped to make the enemy pay a steep price for his victory and to deny him the full fruits of it in the end. But the cost to themselves had been heavy too. They were spent to the limit, worn down to the bone with nothing left inside but the will to go on and the indomitable spirit glinting in their red-rimmed, bloodshot eyes. They desperately needed a break; rest and sleep; but above all they needed for a little while security and at least the illusion of quiet peace. This was what Gavdopula offered them. Here there were no bombs, no whining bullets or flesh-tearing shell-splinters and no chance of a mob of Jerries suddenly appearing round the corner or dropping out of the sky.

Nevertheless sleep wasn't on the agenda. There was too much to be done; and the first thing was to muster the party and count noses.

This little exercise, executed with remarkable speed and efficiency under Josser's orders, revealed that not counting Joe, Josser and himself, Stan had one hundred and five men on his hands instead of the eighty he had bargained for. They were a mixed bag of Australians, British and New Zealanders and included marines, commandos, sappers, gunners and unclassified infantry. Foot-sloggers Josser called them.

"Being unqualified," he explained to Stan, "their duties are varied and they live a very full life. Apart from doing their stint of the fighting, they make roads, dig drains, hump stores, bash spuds, fell trees, clean out the latrines, build huts, erect fences, mount guard and in their spare time polish the brasses on their uniforms. As to privileges, they are entitled to three squares a day, when available, and all the fresh air they can use free. They can also gripe twenty-four hours a day but not too loudly."

From these happy warriors he sorted out one who had a dirty bandage over the left eye and a chronic look of disbelief in the right. Extracting from him the information that his name was Scruffy and that in "civvy street," which seemed to him a million years back, he had run an all-night coffee stall south of the river in London, Josser wished on him the job of cook. With half a dozen helpers, he was to make a fire, improvise utensils and prepare a hot meal for the whole party.

The next step was to list all their resources and measure them against what they had to accomplish.

"We'd better make four piles to start with," suggested Stan, ticking them off on his fingers. "One, all the grub; two, the water containers; three, stores and gear for the scow; and four, all the odds and ends that don't belong with the other three."

This was agreed, and to make it easier Josser marked out and numbered four big well-separated squares on the beach under the cliff. Joe and his plumber's mate were already at work overhauling the engines; but the rest of the mob he divided into two groups. One he sent aboard the lighter to work under Stan; the other was marshaled into four ranks, running from the assembly areas to converge at the inshore end of the brow where he took up his position.

Like everything else he did, the arrangement worked quickly and without a hitch. As each item was handed down the brow, he classified it with a glance, bawled out the number of the pile it belonged to, and grabbed by the leader of the appropriate line, it passed swiftly across the beach to be neatly stowed. Where the stuff was in closed cases or canisters, he made a guess at the nature of the contents and those that baffled him, went on number four —the miscellaneous heap.

The lighter was stripped to her deck-plates and Stan was surprised at the speed with which it was done; then, coming ashore at the end of the operation, he was positively staggered to see what had been made out of the apparently inextricable confusion of worthless old junk that had filled her well. Unloaded, sorted and neatly stacked in a single operation, it not only looked more manageable, but infinitely more valuable for their purpose and his spirits rose considerably at the mere sight of it.

A spring of sweet water had already been located by the cook's mob. It was some distance from the top of the cliff and now all the available hands were concentrated on the job of filling the water containers while Josser and Stan drew up a list of the stores.

They started on the number one heap. The biggest item was canned meat and vegetable stew. Stan made the tally fifty-seven dozen cans.

"That's a lot of stew!" he said.

"We've got a lot of bellies to fill with it," retorted Josser. "What's next?"

"Iron cow. Exactly twelve dozen cans."

"Milk; condensed and sweetened; cans of—one hundred and forty-four," Josser grunted, reading back as he wrote it "Could have done with more of that."

And so on to the end of the list. It wasn't very long but included a fair supply of ship's biscuit packed in sealed cans, a canister of tea, a couple of cases of corned beef, another of tomato ketchup in bottles and a twenty-eight pound box of dried fruit—mixed raisins and sultanas.

The second heap was a matter of simple arithmetic; multiplying the number of each type of container by its capacity and adding up the result revealed that they had storage for two hundred and fifty gallons of water.

"That's half a gallon a nob each day for five days. Should be ample!" said Stan and they moved on to the number three pile.

The most important item here was fuel for the engines. Joe had already worked out the hourly consumption and if his figure was anywhere near right, there was gas for just over fifty hours running. Next came a tool box containing among other things a hammer, handsaw, an assortment of spanners and wrenches, a hatchet, a hank of sail twine, a sail needle and a box of wire nails. Then there was a small tarpaulin used to cover the engines when the scow was not in use, a couple of stout spars, some odds and ends of timber, the mooring wire which had been foul of the propellers, a can of kerosene, a box of Very lights and a pistol for firing them, a watch tackle or handy-billy, a heaving line and a few pieces of cordage of various lengths and thickness. A note was made of the gas but Stan reckoned there was no need to write down the rest and they turned to the last heap of all.

Most of it was useless junk, and when all this had been picked over and rejected, they were left with a big bale done up in burlap, one large wooden case and two smaller ones, the outsides of which gave no indication of their contents.

"Treasure trove!" said Stan. "I bet the big one's full of cigarettes for the mob. That seems to be all we're shy of."

"You've got a hope!" grunted Josser, wrenching open the case with the hatchet. "Look! Matches! Perishing lucifers! —twelve dozen packets of them, I reckon. How many matches does that make at a dozen boxes a packet and fifty to the box?"

"More than we'll ever need! Open up the others quick and let's know the worst."

Josser operated on the remaining two cases. One contained red ink in quart bottles and the other cans of metal polish. Spitting his disgust, he borrowed Stan's sheath-knife and tackled the bale. It held only a bundle of blankets and that was all they got out of the number four heap.

Scruffy now had the grub ready for serving and everybody was knocked off to eat. The stew, boiled up in an old oil drum was dished out into cans which each man picked out of the rubbish dump and scoured to his fancy. Leaving out Stan and Josser, it was the first hot food any of them had eaten for a week and they fairly wolfed it down. Then Scruffy produced a brew of tea sweetened with condensed milk. It was thick enough to skate on and, used undiluted, would have done a good job as a paint-stripper; but it made their day.

The meal finished, everybody turned to again and the stores and filled water-containers were humped back aboard the lighter to be carefully stowed under Stan's supervision.

There were two sergeants and three corporals among the men lifted off the beach at Sphakia. Josser now called these out to a conference with Joe, Stan and himself and turned the rest loose to spend the remainder of the afternoon cleaning themselves up.

"Now, Stan!" said Josser when the conference was assembled and he had voted himself into the chair. "You open the ball. How do you think we're doing? I reckon myself it's going like a bomb."

"Yes, I know; but don't let that fool you. We've still got one hundred and eighty miles of open sea to cross. That's not far, given the right kind of craft to do it in; but it could be a long way for this old scow packed to her gunwales with men."

Having nipped Josser's uprush of optimism in the bud, Stan went on with some arithmetic. As he said, it was roughly a hundred and eighty miles to Tobruk, but allowing for drift and yaw it would be safer to call it two hundred. At five knots that was forty hours flat. They had petrol for fifty which gave them ten hours in hand, so it should be easy. On the other hand, however, they had no compass, chart, sextant or aid to navigation of any kind, and the landing craft was designed to work inshore. Her function was to ferry men between a beach and vessels at anchor off it and she had neither the shape, power, nor equipment for a deep-sea passage. Being flat-bottomed and square-ended both fore and aft, she steered badly and with the wind anywhere on the beam would go sideways like a crab. On top of that there was no shelter in her from sun or weather and the men, sitting perforce on her deck, would be grilled like sausages on a hot plate if the sky remained unclouded by day. Nevertheless, he was confident he could make a course, steering by the stars through the night and by the sun during the day.

"Starting tonight just after dark to dodge the *Luftwaffe*," he concluded, "I reckon we should make a landfall somewhere on the other side about sundown the day after tomorrow. If our luck and the weather hold, that is."

"And if it breaks?" demanded Joe. "The weather I mean?"

"That's one of the chances we've got to take," put in Josser. "On full rations we've got enough grub and water for three days; but on a low diet we could last out three weeks. We'll cut the issue to a quarter right from the start just to be safe."

Stan had other worries besides food. From Joe he learned that though the engines functioned, they were badly worn and desperately in need of overhaul. Suppose they conked, he thought. Suppose he had overestimated the speed and she did only three knots instead of five. That would put them out of juice still fifty miles short of the African coast, or anyhow too far off it to swim. Suppose the sea got up and the old scow, lacking the longitudinal strength to ride it, buckled amidships then folded end to

end. Suppose they encountered a prowling Italian war-
ship or were spotted by some wide-ranging Heinkel or
Stuka. And biggest worry of all, suppose he made a muck-
up of the course and they never fetched!

He had the sense to keep his headaches to himself however and they moved on to the division and allocation of
responsibility. Dividing it up was easy, for the standard
shipboard pattern of departments—deck, engine-room and
victualing—applied even here; and after a brief discussion,
one of the sergeants, an Australian called Steadman and
appropriately nicknamed Slasher, was put in charge of
the food. Working with him he would have the other
sergeant, a tight-packed bandy-legged little Welshman
named Prosser, to issue the water. Joe Clitterhouse and
the plumber were given the engines to work between
them in whatever way suited them best. That left the deck
department and Josser was unanimously elected mate.

He had many of the qualities that go to make a good
executive officer; he was methodical, clever with his hands
and had a flare for improvisation; he could see and move
like a cat in the dark, was soft-spoken and understanding
but tough enough to come out of any sort of roughhouse
on top; he could handle men either with kid gloves or the
other way and, above all, he was completely unflappable.

The general control of the lighter and all her company
would be in his hands. He would have to see she was kept
clean and tidy. This was a very important point with so
many people crammed into such a small space and no bogs
aboard; and if she ran into trouble it would become more
important with each day the passage was prolonged. He
would be responsible for the safety and well being of all
hands and their good behavior, settling any disagreements
and breaking up any arguments among them before they

started bashing each other about. He would also see none of them went over the wall through walking where they had no right to be, and if some clumsy clot did get his feet crossed and finished up in the drink, he would organize the rescue. Finally, he would do watch and watch with Stan.

"That brings us to the last thing," said Josser. "With over a hundred brains of assorted sizes and brilliance working on our problems, we're going to have more ideas about how to run this scow than a shaggy dog's got fleas; so somebody must be daddy of us all. You can call him O.C., skipper or anything else you like, but he'll make the decisions and whatever he says must go for everybody. Agreed?"

"Agreed," said Stan and the others having nodded their approval, he went on. "So far as I can see, there's only one man for it and that's yourself, Josser."

"There's only one man for it, all right," answered Josser, "but I'm not even a candidate. It's you."

"Me! Oh, for Pete's sake, come off it! Why me? I'm only a kid."

"Maybe, but war has a way of sorting out men from boys before the hair on their chests has even begun to sprout. Look, Stan! you're the only one in the bunch who can tell a bollard from a bar of soap. You know how to find the way by the sun and the stars and I'll back your nose for it when there's neither. You know the sea and its ways. I mean when it cuts up rough you can tell whether it's just fooling around a bit or likely to get really dicey and what to do about it. And because you know ships, you've already learned more about this perishing old tin can than all the rest of us would pick up from now till the cows come home; what she'll stand and what she won't;

it. After that we'll top up the water containers and get ready to sail as soon as the light goes."

"Okay, skipper! You'll do fine!" Josser grinned, punched him lightly in the chest then hurried ashore to pass on the word.

But there was no rest for Stan. He had too much on his mind. Instead of finding a soft spot in the shade and curling up, he went slowly over the landing craft from bow to stern; not checking up or anything like that but just trying to get the size and shape and feel of her into his bones. He was still at it when Scruffy signaled that supper was ready.

Going ashore to eat with the others, he examined both sea and sky and liked the look of neither. The wind had died away completely during the afternoon, and the sea was now oily smooth and brassy where it reflected the afterglow of the sunset; and all along the horizon from west through north to the already darkling east, cloud masses shaped like the toppling crags of a nightmare landscape were piling up. Something was brewing and he could only hope it would take a long time to mature—forty hours, to be precise.

when to nurse her and when to drive her and the best way
to do both. So I'm telling you, if ever we get to Africa
it'll be you that takes us there. But responsibility and
authority go together; whichever comes first carries the
other with it and you can't separate them. From now on
you're skipper and it's all yours."

Stan, while not underestimating in any way what they
were up against, thought Josser was suffering from a rush
of organization to the head and getting the whole expedi
tion out of proportion. After all, they weren't preparing to
sail the Atlantic or circumnavigate the globe but only to
cross a strip of the Mediterranean to Africa. It was a two
day passage and he was talking as if they were embarking
on a two-year voyage.

"All right!" retorted Josser. "But we'll still play it my
way. Then if the luck holds and we make it in under three
days, you can laugh your heads off at me and I'll join in
but if anything busts loose to make us longer than that, we
won't be caught with our pants down."

And that was it. Stan, more than a little embarrassed
and still only half convinced of the necessity for the
decision, reluctantly accepted it and took over his first
command.

Ashore, the troops had done what was possible in the
way of cleaning themselves up. As there was neither
cake of soap, a razor nor a pair of scissors among the lot
of them, it wasn't much. They were still ragged and shaggy
but they didn't smell so powerfully; not to windward
anyhow.

"We'll rest them up now, till sundown," said Stan, giving
his first order to Josser. "Then we'll have a last brew up
and maybe a sandwich of biscuit and bully beef to go with

CHAPTER 11

THE landing craft sailed from Gavdopula at nightfall and
of all the things that really mattered this was the last
one to go according to plan; not through anybody slipping
up or because the planning itself was cockeyed, but simply
because, when it came to the push, it was their luck, not
the fuel, that ran out on them first.

When they had got her clear of the island, Stan picked
out the Pole Star and headed south by keeping it dead
astern. He took the first watch himself so he could check
her steering and general behavior and work out ways of
correcting them. There was still no wind to speak of and
the sea was smooth; but the old scow made the swell seem
quite heavy. It was running down from the northwest and
she had it on her starboard quarter which gave her an
awkward lurching movement, neither pitch nor roll and
completely unpredictable. Every time her stern lifted and
she heeled to port her head swung round that way and
constant effort was demanded to keep her on course.

"How's she going?" asked Josser, relieving him at midnight.

"Not too badly, I suppose, considering the shape of her and what she was built for. But you'll have to watch her all the time or she'll be heading back to Sphakia before you can say knife."

He waited till he was sure Josser had the hang of it, then got his head down; and in spite of the uneasy movement, the discomfort and the weight of responsibility he carried, slept solidly and dreamlessly until he was called again at 4 A.M.

A chill little breeze was now blowing out of the north and although the sky was still clear overhead with Polaris plainly visible astern, the cloud masses banked along the horizon were all in motion. Nothing else was changed and Josser was inclined to give his natural optimism an airing.

"Well, she's still afloat and the engines haven't packed up on us yet," he said. "I begin to think it might be a piece of cake after all."

"Could be; but I'm not putting the flags out till I know what speed she's doing," Stan retorted. "How do you think the happy warriors are making out in the well?"

"I've heard a few of them throwing up in the night so I reckon they aren't exactly crazy about the motion; but nobody's decided to get out and walk."

Stan grinned in the darkness and leaving Josser to bed down under the bulwarks, gave all his attention to the steering; but when day broke and the condition of the lighter and the men aboard her was revealed, he felt more like puking himself than grinning. With so many men to carry in so little space, careful planning had been needed to get them stowed. Just to ensure they weren't lying on top of each other wasn't enough. There had to be room left for anyone who felt the need, to be able to move without putting his foot in some other fellow's mouth and in addition a reasonable gangway had to be left along the whole length of the deck. The problem had been solved by arranging the men in four lines running fore and aft, the two outside ranks sitting with their backs against the bulwark and the inside ones back to back facing outboard. They were still more or less in that position; but at least every second man was seasick and, leaving the smell out of it altogether, the sight of the deck alone would have made a pig's stomach turn.

For the sake of morale as well as comfort and common decency something had to be done about it without delay and Stan reluctantly roused Josser from his much needed rest. He in turn sorted out Sergeant Prosser, who claimed providence had endowed him with a copper-bottomed stomach and no sense of smell. Together they segregated the sick to leeward and instructed them in the art of spewing without being antisocial; then they organized the tougher elements into a sanitary squad and cleaned up the mess.

When they had finished, Stan turned the wheel over to Josser and, going forward, threw an empty food can overboard. As it floated past he walked aft, keeping abreast of it.

"How fast does a man walk?" he asked, halting alongside Josser and watching the can drift away astern.

"Depends on the man and where he's going."

"This is an average bloke and it felt like he was going to a funeral."

"That's three miles an hour, then. Not more. Why do you ask?"

"I've been checking up and that's roughly the speed we're making." Stan stared ahead and did some mental arithmetic. Fifty hours at three knots was a hundred and fifty miles; so at the rate they were going the engines would conk for want of fuel at least thirty miles short of the African coast. It wouldn't do, not by a jugful, and suddenly he swung round. "Look Josser! We've got to rig some sort of sail. There's a fair wind. It might give us an extra couple of knots but in any case a sail would steady her and we'd get more out of the engines."

"I see your point; but what will you use for canvas? The tail of your shirt?"

"We've got a tarpaulin and a couple of spars. You keep her going and I'll see to it."

With Sergeant Prosser and half a dozen helpers, Stan got busy. First they sorted out the spars, selecting the bigger and stouter of the two for the mast. Then they spread out the tarpaulin. It was designed to cover the engines when the scow was laid up and there were brass eyelets along all four edges of it.

"That makes it easier," said Stan. "We'll lace the top edge on to the yard all the way along and I'll splice the sheets into the eyelets at the bottom corners."

This was done and the only real problem left was devising a step for the mast. In the end Stan solved it by setting up the spar against the brow and tomming off the heel of it with a plank running athwartships. The ends of the plank were jammed off between the forward bulwark stanchion and the brow on either side; then stays already attached to the head of the spar were set up and the yard with the sail laced to it was hoisted.

As a rig everything about it was crude and makeshift and the mast raked forward at such an angle that the foot of the sail was away out ahead of the scow altogether; but it worked. Going aft when he had adjusted the sheets, Stan checked her speed with another empty can and this time he had to hurry to keep pace with it. She was much steadier too which was going to make a big difference to the men packed in the well.

And now it was the turn of the weather to go sour on them. The wind, still out of the north, had steadily increased during the morning. By noon it was at least force five which, now they had a sail rigged, was all to the good for it drove her along handsomely; but it continued to freshen and the sea rose with it. Meanwhile, the sky had become completely overcast and Stan was making his course by holding her right before the wind, trusting the movement of the clouds would warn him of any change in its direction while it was still pending.

At sundown it was blowing a moderate gale and there was no more comfort aboard the lighter for anybody as she ran before it. Because the sail was so far forward, the pressure of wind in it tended to push her down by the head. So, each time she plunged, the square bow hit the sea with a tremendous smack and the spray, flung high by the impact, smothered the whole length of her. The deck was awash and every man aboard soaked to the skin, worn-out and bone-weary with the incessant jerking movement. But still Stan kept her going, counting the time gained and the ground covered more valuable than the comfort lost.

Twenty-four hours out, he made his reckoning. Taking into account everything he could think of, he calculated they had covered ninety-two miles.

"That leaves a hundred and eight miles to go," he said to Josser. "Twenty-one hours at five knots—if we can keep it up."

That was Stan's worry now; keeping it up and measuring the need to do so against the risks involved; and he didn't even try to sleep that night but watched her every minute of it. Beside him, Josser fretted about the crazy, plunging motion, thinking she might bust herself open and fall apart; but Stan knew the danger lay elsewhere and he kept his knowledge to himself.

It was the shape of her, the square, chopped-off stern that bothered him. To run safely in a heavy following sea, a vessel needs to be cunningly shaped aft so that she yields to the first upsurge of each wave then lifts smoothly with it, keeping her course and letting it pass squarely under her. She has to go with the sea and ride it. But all the landing craft could do was to squat sullenly and be thrown about by it. Stan's fear was that she might go on squatting and the sea break over her; and he gambled on the sail holding her dead straight before wind and sea.

He was greatly relieved when the new day broke. Though it brought no change in the weather and the sea was if anything running higher than ever, they could at least see what it was doing and there was that much less chance of it taking them unaware. Again in the gray dawn, he weighed their progress against the risks involved. The alternative to running was to stream some kind of sea anchor out ahead and ride to it with the engines throttled back until the sea went down; but that meant using fuel they couldn't spare, drifting at a speed and in a direction he had no means of calculating and above all, losing time. One glance at the men, packed on the streaming deck of the lighter decided him. Some of them were already in a bad way and time was the one thing he couldn't afford to lose. He kept her going.

Soon afterwards, as if to confirm his decision, the sky rifted low down in the east and the sun rode up into the gap; then the clouds began to move, slowly rolling back on themselves towards the northwestern and southwestern horizons. By mid-morning the wind had turned squally and eased considerably, though it was still fierce in the gusts and the sea continued to run dangerously high for the unwieldy old scow. Nevertheless, she was running much easier and they began to congratulate themselves on having weathered the worst of it.

That was the moment when the accident which Stan had been dreading for twenty-four hours happened. It was a squall, screaming down on them out of the north, that caused it and though he saw it coming there was nothing he could do about it. Striking squarely aft, it swept the length of the scow and hit the makeshift sail like a wall. The mast and stays held but the canvas split with a crack like a rifle shot and streamed to leeward in rags and tatters on the wind. Released from the steadying pressure of the sail, her head reared up and at the same time she heeled and swung away to port. Stan gave her all the helm he could to check the yaw but she didn't answer and glancing aft, he saw her stern dug deep and a great sea lifting high above it.

"Look out!" he yelled, and a moment later the sea broke inboard and engulfed her.

That could well have been the end of it for them all. Filled to the gunwales with water and still heeling crazily, it was odds on she would either founder or capsize; but she did neither. Instead she lifted, righting herself and emptying as she came. It seemed like a miracle but Stan was too busy even to wonder about it and when he had her under control again, he saw immediately what had happened to save her. The sea, crashing along the deck, had struck the hinged brow at the fore-end, and parting the lashings, forced it open, thus making a gap through which she had emptied just in time.

"Somebody's guardian angel must be working overtime," said Josser. "But where do we go from here?"

"First we've got to make sure it doesn't happen again," answered Stan. "You take the wheel. I'm going forward to stream some sort of sea anchor. We'll count noses and reckon up the damage when she's safe."

There was no lack of willing hands and under his direction the now useless mast and yard were quickly struck and lashed together. A short length of rope was then hitched to each end of the bundle, forming a bridle to which Stan bent the stoutest line available. He checked the lashings, took a couple of turns with the line round a stanchion—then had the spars lifted and dumped over the side. They immediately began to stream away ahead and he paid out the line until only a fathom or so was left with which he finally fastened it off on the stanchion.

All this time, the scow had been throwing about alarmingly—so much so it was impossible to stand without holding on; but the pull of the drogue ahead steadied her immediately, and feeling a little easier in his mind, Stan now began a survey of the damage.

Thanks to his warning shout nobody had been caught completely unaware by the boarding sea and Sergeant Prosser, having called the roll, was able to report all present. He added that some of the men had been knocked about a bit but none of them seriously hurt. This was good hearing and on top of it Stan decided, after making a closer examination, that the damaged brow could be yanked back into place with the watch tackle.

So far, so good; but the rest of it could hardly have been worse, for as the sea swept through her it had taken with it most of their carefully hoarded stores and equipment. A case of corned beef and a few tins of milk were all the food left to them and of water there were only two five-gallon cans.

Trying to conceal his dismay and anxiety, Stan called the N.C.O.'s aft for another conference.

"Now here's the position," he said when he had told them about the loss of the food and water. "We're forty hours out and should have only about thirty miles to go. But that's if we've made a straight course which I'm sure we haven't. I reckon it's nearer fifty and could be more. Now according to Joe, we've fuel left for ten hours' running——"

"Well then," interrupted Josser, "what are we worrying about? That should just about do it."

"Should's the right word," said Stan. "It should do it if we make five knots all the way but it leaves us with nothing in hand if we don't. Now the sail's gone I know she'll only do five knots in a smooth sea, so I'm going to cut the engines and let her ride to that drogue till the sea goes down. What drift she makes will be to the southward, so we won't lose anything by it; only time. I've been trying to save that but we've got to let it go now."

"What about the grub and the water?" asked Sergeant Prosser.

"To be on the safe side, work out what's left to last four days."

Nobody questioned Stan's decisions and the engines were stopped right away. The sea anchor, crude as it was, proved effective and though the lighter's movement was still extremely uncomfortable, it was less violent and she was no longer inclined to swing off the sea into the trough. So when the damage to the brow had been made good as far as was possible and the deck squared up again, they settled down to wait.

Stan hoped to get under way by nightfall but during the afternoon the wind backed and freshened from the west. It didn't reach gale force this time but it was strong enough to pile up the sea again and he was forced to abandon the idea. At daybreak on the 4th the weather was foul again and the sea running as high as ever.

They were then sixty hours out from Gavdopula and everybody was feeling the effects of the cramped conditions, short rations and exposure. Some of the men, notably those who had carried the rough end of the retreat to Sphakia, were in a bad way and Stan sweated his guts out about them. The sight of their suffering tempted him to throw caution to the winds and make a dash for it; but his instincts as well as his reasoning mind told him he was doing right to wait and he resisted the urge.

Soon after dawn, the sky cleared again and throughout the morning the heat of the blazing sun grew fiercer as the wind dropped away. By noon it was roasting hot on the deck and the whole company was suffering severely from thirst; but still he held on. Among the few items left by the boarding sea was the bale of blankets and now he had these broken out and issued to the men.

"Souse them in the drink," he said, "then rig them over your heads as best you can to keep off the sun."

"How much longer?" asked Sergeant Prosser, trying to moisten his cracked lips with a tongue like a piece of old leather. "It would help them to know."

"Tell them sundown unless the wind comes away again," answered Stan, resuming his study of sea and sky. He had started the passage with a truckload of fears—hostile planes, prowling enemy warships, the lighter's total lack of seaworthiness, the innumerable possibilities of going wrong with his course and so on—but now they were all concentrated into the single overriding dread of the weather; and through that long sweltering afternoon he watched every wisp of cloud and every movement of the sea as if their lives depended on it.

But conditions continued to improve and at nightfall he decided it was worthwhile getting under way. Time and effort would have been saved by cutting the sea anchor adrift but he insisted on recovering it and with some difficulty it was hauled aboard. Then a hoarse cheer went up as the engines were started and the old scow began to punch and batter her way south once more.

She was seventy-two hours out and to the men aboard her it already seemed more like seventy-two days.

"Look at those stars!" croaked Josser. "It's a fine night and she's going like a bomb. I reckon the jinx must have gone overboard with the grub. Ten hours more! That's dawn tomorrow."

The jinx, however, was still with them and round about eleven o'clock Stan, who had the first watch, began to have difficulty keeping her on a straight course. All along it had been necessary to carry a certain amount of starboard helm to correct her tendency to swing off to port and now he found it needed more and more. The most puzzling thing about it was that the tendency varied a great deal, sometimes being relatively slight and sometimes quite pronounced. He racked his brains for an explanation but couldn't find one, and was on the point of calling Josser to take over so he could investigate when Joe Clitterhouse loomed up alongside him out of the night.

"More trouble, Stan!" he said. "Flipping clutch slipping."

"Which engine?"

"Port."

"I see." Stan chewed at his bottom lip. This not only

accounted for her pulling away off course but also meant she was losing power, burning up precious fuel to no purpose at all, and he blamed himself bitterly for not having tumbled to it long since. That however was going to butter no parsnips for anybody and he turned to Joe. "Can you fix it?"

"Sure. Come daybreak. Can't work in the dark. But it's going to take time."

"Time," said Stan grimly, "is what we can least afford to lose now the sea's going down, so you'd better stop her and get cracking right away. I'll rig up some sort of light for you to work by."

"Okay, kid! You're the guv'nor!" said Joe, then swinging round he cut the engines, and losing way, the battered landing craft once more lay like a hulk, pitching and rolling uneasily and unpredictably to the unseen swell.

CHAPTER 12

T HIS latest setback was a bitter blow to everybody aboard
the lighter and it weighed most heavily on the men
packed in the well of her, because for them there was
nothing to do except wait. But they were down to funda-
mentals now. Having opted for freedom and staked their
lives on a blind chance of getting it, there wasn't much
point in bellyaching about the delay. It was part of the
price, like the hunger and thirst, the cramp and extreme
discomfort, and they paid it without complaint.

It was easier for Stan because he had time neither for
brooding about what had happened nor for wondering
what would go next. His first problem was to provide Joe
with enough light to work by and he roped in Josser to
help.

"There's still some rags of canvas flapping about that
spar up forward," he said. "Cut a bit of it free and draw
out the threads. It's cotton, and I want four bundles of
them about eight inches long and as thick as your little
finger to make wicks."

Next he took a tin of condensed milk, and working

mostly by feel in the dark, punched two holes in the top of it; one in the center roughly three-eighths of an inch in diameter and the other near the rim very much smaller. Blowing into the tin through the smaller hole he forced all the milk out through the bigger one, catching it in a spare container, and then refilled the can with kerosene. By the time he had treated four cans in this way, Josser had enough threads of canvas drawn to make the first wick which was worked into one of the cans through the center hole, leaving about half an inch protruding. Plugging the hole on the rim with a matchstick, Stan put a light to the wick. He wasn't at all sure it would burn and it didn't at first; but after a moment of despair he realized the end of the wick was still dry. He primed it by up-ending the can and tried again. This time it flared then settled to a reasonably steady flame which threw about as much light as a single tallow candle.

Having proved his idea, Stan quickly finished off the other three cans, and disposing them around the engine to the best advantage, Joe got busy on the faulty clutch.

This conquest of the darkness was like a shot in the arm to everybody. It not only saved them hours of frustration and uncertainty but renewed their confidence in themselves and their purpose. Above all, it seemed to prove their ability to beat the odds and when Joe got her going again, the cheer that went up was good to hear. There was still something of defiance in it but more of sureness and no hint at all of desperation.

The dawn was breaking when Stan brought her back on to the course for Africa and it revealed the best weather conditions they had so far encountered. The sea was smooth and though the northerly swell persisted it had lengthened and flattened considerably. In consequence, the movement of the scow was slower and for the first time had a predictable rhythm about it. She steered better too and the chug of the engines had a deeper, more satisfying note. A faint haze blurred the horizon but overhead the sky was clear and there was only the whisper of a breeze, variable in direction but mainly westerly.

"When do we start looking for something?" demanded Josser, giving his rising optimism a loose rein.

"The horizon isn't too clear but we should be able to pick up the land about ten miles off." Stan did some reckoning. "*When* is a different question. It depends on what sort of course we've made."

"All right then; give us both the long and the short of it."

"At the best I should say within the next hour and at the worst in another four."

That was near enough for Josser, and going forward, he draped himself across the top of the brow and began looking. His optimism quickly spread and soon the fore-end of the scow was lined with eager men, watching the edge of the sea for the smudge that would be their first sight of Africa.

At eight o'clock, Sergeants Prosser and Steadman issued the morning rations. They were down to a cubic inch of corned beef and half a cupful of water per man now. One or two nibbled and sipped at it, tormenting themselves to make it last; but mostly they swallowed the meat like a pill and took the water in a single gulp to wash it down, then resumed their vigil.

They were still watching and still hoping at ten o'clock. The horizon was sharp and clear now and even Stan was beginning to tell himself it couldn't be much longer when Joe suddenly lined up alongside him.

"See anything yet?" he asked, his face as blank and his voice as expressionless as ever.

"No. Not a thing."

"Better be soon," said Joe. "The juice; last of it's in the tank. Want to save it?"

"Not much point in that," answered Stan after a moment's thought. "We can't be far off now, so keep her going."

On she went, mile after mile and still the sharp line of the horizon ahead remained unbroken. Minute by minute now, the tension aboard her was mounting and nobody felt it more acutely than Stan. The responsibility was his and he didn't want anybody to carry the can for him; so he wasn't only watching, but also listening to the putter of the engines, dreading the first break in the steady beat that would signal the end of the fuel; and his mind was racing back, reckoning and re-reckoning in an effort to convince himself he hadn't boobed. Between whiles he checked the course by the time and the position of the sun. Over and over again he did it and always it was dead on.

Then just on noon, abruptly and without warning the engines died. A moment or two later, the way was off her and she lay, once more a helpless hulk, the packed ranks on her deck turned their staring eyes from the empty horizon towards Stan while the silence built up around her.

There was something terrifying about the sudden stillness. It held the lighter and everybody aboard her like a spell and Stan felt it sucking out his courage and the will to go on. He knew it was doing the same for everybody else and tried to force himself into action; but the disappointment was too big. It weighed him down, heart and limbs, and the fact that it had been on the cards all along made it no easier to carry now.

How long this frozen stillness lasted, Stan had no idea. It was Joe who moved first and broke the silence.

"Listen!" he said, grabbing Stan's arm. "Hear anything?"

With an effort, Stan jerked up his head. For a moment he heard only the beat of his own blood, then he caught another sound. It was the throbbing drone of aircraft engines and, swinging round, he searched the sky astern, finally locating the plane low down to the westward.

"Coming towards us," said Joe. "Might be one of ours."

"And it might not. We'll take no chances!" Functioning freely now in mind and body, Stan turned back inboard and barked out his instructions. "Flat on deck everybody. Cover yourselves up with the blankets and don't move!"

The men jumped to it and in a matter of seconds they had vanished. All that could be seen by anybody looking down on the lighter was a flat expanse of dirty gray which even the keenest-eyed pilot would take to be an empty deck.

"He might not spot us," said Stan, crouching beside Joe under the canopy aft. "But if he does, he'll think the scow's derelict and sheer off."

Joe grunted unintelligibly. He was watching the approaching aircraft and suddenly he dug Stan in the ribs.

"Relax, kid!" he said. "One of ours."

"You're sure of that?"

"Certain. She's a Blenheim. Can't mistake them."

This discovery altered the whole situation, though it was a moment or two before either of them realized the full implications of it. When the penny did drop, Stan jumped as if he had been stung and let go a yell so full of wild excitement it brought the men out from cover even quicker than they had gone under it. They saw what was cooking immediately and the excitement swept through them like a bomb blast. The fear now was that the pilot would miss them and they were suddenly aware of the smallness of the landing craft in relation to the enormous expanse of water on which she floated. From the height at which the plane was flying she couldn't have been much more than a speck. Nevertheless, they waved the blankets frantically and shouted their heads off.

"Looks like he's going to miss us!" said Josser, staring upwards. The aircraft was almost overhead now and still flying steadily to the eastward. "The perisher must be blind!"

"He's a long way up and we're not much to see." The great uprush of hope was already beginning to recede in Stan and he clutched at it desperately. "If only we had some sort of signal; a couple of flares or a rocket!"

"We have!" Josser snapped his fingers, dived in under the canopy and emerged dragging a wooden box. "I just remembered it! The Very lights! Help me get it open."

Joe snatched up a hammer and with a few shrewd wallops knocked the box to pieces. As it fell adrift, Josser grabbed the pistol and in five seconds flat had loosed off three of the flares. He fired them on a high trajectory so they would be the maximum time in the air and though the light they gave was green and almost invisible in the bright sunshine, they shed a very satisfactory trail of white smoke. But the Blenheim gave no sign and flew on.

"Try another couple!" said Joe. "Throw the flipping box at him!"

"No, wait!" Stan put a hand on Josser's arm. "He must have seen that. Give him time."

As he spoke, the starboard wing of the plane began to dip and, banking steeply, she came round in a tight turn then swooped back over the landing craft. Three times she circled coming lower each time until she was no more than a hundred feet above the water.

"He's seen us!" yelled Josser to the packed ranks on the deck. "Wave now, you pie-faced dead-beats, wave and shout your perishing heads off!"

The men needed no encouragement. They were fairly lit up now, capering like a bunch of dancing dervishes, waving blankets, rifles, shirts, anything that came to hand, whistling, hooting, cheering and between whiles slapping each other on the back.

Stan was still watching the plane. As it circled the third time, the pilot stuck out his hand and made the thumbs-up sign; then he waggled his wings, swung round on to a westerly course and roared away, climbing steeply as he went.

"Well, I reckon that's it!" said Josser when the Blenheim had disappeared. "What's the time?"

"Twelve-fifteen."

"Is that all? Takes you to the perishing fair, doesn't it? A quarter of an hour ago we were down the drain just waiting for the plug to be pulled and now, here we are— as good as home and dried!"

According to his thinking the Blenheim wouldn't use his radio for fear of alerting the jackals; but he was most likely based on Tobruk and as soon as he landed there would report the position of the landing craft. The information would be passed on to the naval authorities in the harbor and they would send out some sort of craft to tow the old scow in.

"How far are we off Tobruk?" he demanded.

"I don't know exactly." Stan scratched his head and tried to work it out. "Anything up to a hundred miles, I should say."

"Well then, they'll send something fast for sure. An M.L., that's my bet. They do about thirty-five. Allow an hour for them to get weaving and three for the journey and call it four o'clock. It'll be all over then but the shouting."

"Hope you're right!" said Stan. It seemed too good to be true and yet he could see no snags. The landing craft had been sighted and identified, but that wasn't all. The pilot of the Blenheim had flown close enough to get a rough idea of the number of men aboard her and their condition; this would be included in his report and ensure immediate action on it. So, even if Josser's estimate of the timing was a trifle optimistic, they would be safe by nightfall at the latest and if it took whatever arrived another twenty-four hours to tow them into Tobruk that wouldn't matter because she'd be sure to bring food and water with her.

This line of reasoning made any uneasiness seem just plain stupidity and he settled down with the rest to wait.

At three thirty he posted lookouts and at four took the binoculars himself, climbing on to the engine canopy to get the widest possible view. From south through west to north the sea was still empty, the hard line of the horizon unbroken. But there was time enough yet and he refused to worry. At five, in spite of all the arguments he could muster to hold it at bay, the uneasiness began to creep up on him again and when the sun went down with still nothing in sight he began to sweat.

"The perishers are taking their time about it, aren't they!" said Josser, impatient for once in his life. "What'll we do if they don't show up by nightfall? We'll want some finding in the dark."

"That'll be okay." Stan had already worked this one out. "We've got the Very lights. There's twenty-one of them left, so we can fire one every half hour."

"Half an hour's a long time. How about if they come just after we've fired one and have gone again before we put up the next?"

"They won't." Stan shook his head. "These things go up well over a hundred feet. At a hundred and twenty the horizon is about twelve miles off. That means they would have to cover twenty-four miles in under half an hour to miss both. Even your M.L. won't do that sort of speed."

"You make it sound all right, but I've got a funny feeling, Stan."

"Okay, Jeremiah! You're not the only one; but I'm sitting on mine till daybreak anyhow."

The night shut down on them soon after this. It was fine and clear with no wind to speak of and the sea smooth and still; the sort of night when sounds travel far and a man's cough or the sudden click of his heel on a deck-plate plucks painfully at the nerves. Stan changed his lookouts at short intervals but it was a mere formality because every man who could find room had his arms hooked over the bulwarks and was staring outboard with his ears flapping, and nobody even thought of sleep.

"I've been thinking," said Josser when Stan fired the first flare. "If the perishing *Luftwaffe* spots one of those, he'll be here with his boots blacked to investigate."

"You don't have to tell me!" snapped Stan. "It's a chance we've got to take, so keep your fingers crossed."

When midnight came and there was still no sign of the rescue craft, Stan in his own mind finally decided there wasn't going to be one. He kept on firing the flares at thirty-minute intervals so the men would have what comfort there was in seeing them go up and feeling something was being done; but he knew now it was hopeless. The Blenheim must have ditched on the way back and the weight of responsibility was on him again. There was no way of evading it; the next move was his, and between whiles he worked it out.

The dawn seemed a long time coming and its reluctant light revealed nothing but the empty sea. Then in ones and twos and little groups, as the hope died in them, the men turned inboard and looked towards Stan. At the sight of their ravaged faces, their sunken staring eyes, his courage almost failed him. Not because they were despairing; they weren't; nor asking. But just trusting; looking to him. He pulled himself together and called the N.C.O.'s to another conference which, though he didn't know it, was to be the last.

"I think we ought to get under way again as soon as can be," he began, getting down to brass tacks immediately.

"It's all right talking," said Josser. "But how? We're right out of gas and there isn't even a perishing sail now."

"No, but we've still got a bale of blankets and there's a hank of twine in the toolbox. We can make one."

"And what about the Blenheim?" demanded Sergeant Prosser. "I mean to say, once we shift from here they'll never find us."

"If you ask me, they aren't even going to start looking." Stan leaned forward. "Let's face it! It's eighteen hours now since that Blenheim sighted us; time enough for any sort of powered craft to get out here from Tobruk and back again. But nothing's showed up and it's my bet the Blenheim didn't make it. That passes the buck back to us."

"Maybe you're right, but you don't know. Where's the harm in waiting a bit longer?"

"How long? Don't you see we're all growing weaker and every hour counts. We've got to make the coast while we've still got the strength to work the old scow and we can't afford to wait."

The Welshman was still inclined to gamble on the Blenheim; but Stan finally overcame his doubts by pointing out that it would take some time to make and rig the sail and even when they got under way their progress would be very slow; so in any case it would be several hours before they got clear of the area in which the aircraft had sighted them.

They got down to it then. The strongest among the men were sorted out to handle the spars and a space was cleared on the deck where Stan could work. Checking the total area of blankets available, he found it added up to roughly four times that of the tarpaulin lost in the gale. But that had been quite big enough and after some thought he decided to make the new sail the same shape and size, using a double thickness of blanket to give it strength.

He didn't rush the job. There was no sense in sticking up something which the first puff of wind would rip to shreds; and making it strong took time. When he had the sail shaped, he roped all four edges of it, leaving loops at the bottom corners and sewing a length of line across each diagonal. Then he quilted the two thicknesses of blanket together with criss-crossing rows of stitches and it was ready for lacing to the yard. He used the tarred hemp heaving line for this, weaving it through the lay of the roping on the upper edge; and when this had been done to his satisfaction, he spliced the sheets into the loops on the corners.

All the time his fingers worked, his mind was juggling with figures: adding, subtracting, multiplying, dividing;

setting total miles to go against distance run; engine speed against leeway and drift. It was all guesswork and he knew it; but the longer he mucked about with it the stronger grew the feeling in him that the land was just out of sight below the horizon. Ten miles more; maybe fifteen; say twenty at the outside; and so on until he had almost convinced himself he could smell it!

Meanwhile Josser's mob had set the mast up as before and late in the afternoon the yard was hoisted. At the sight of it going up another wave of hope swept through the old scow; but it ebbed quicker than it made, for the wind wasn't strong enough to fill the sail and it hung flapping idly against the makeshift mast.

"Okay!" said Stan, setting his jaw and looking at the sky. "It'll freshen a bit after sundown, sucking in towards the land as the heat goes up out of the desert."

He was riding a hunch now; or maybe the hunch was riding him; but either way he knew all through his bones this was their last throw and was determined to put everything they had left on it. Setting Josser to sort out enough timber and cordage to rig another mast and yard, he got busy with the rest of the blankets and made them up into a second sail. Having the hang of it now, he worked faster, but he was still at it when the night shut down and finished by the smoky light of Joe Clitterhouse's duck-lamps.

Meanwhile, confirming his forecast, the breeze had freshened. It was filling the crude sail forward and the old scow had way on her again; but not enough to steer by.

Hanging on grimly to his belief in his ability to beat the odds, Stan had the second sail hoisted on a mast stepped just forward of the engines. That filled too, and the lapping of the water against her square bow quickened a little. She was heading nearly due east with the wind, such as it was, broad on her port beam. Hopefully he put the helm hard over and waited for her to come round to the southward; but still she didn't respond.

"What's up, kid?" demanded Joe. "Won't she play?"

"No. The ugly old scow! There's no life nor lift in her. She's all square; not a curve for the sea to work on."

"But she is moving!"

"Yes. Sideways like a crab. From the feel of her it would take a tug to shift her head. A tug——" Stan broke off and turned to Josser. He was suddenly alert again and his voice when he found it was tense with excitement. "That's it! She won't come on her own so she's got to be pushed. Do you think we've got the manpower to do it?"

"All the way to Africa? Tall order, isn't it?"

"No, no. Only on to her course. Don't you see? Once she's round with the wind dead astern and the sails trimmed, she'll stay like that. And she'll go faster into the bargain."

"We could try it," said Josser without conviction.

He explained to the men what was afoot and called for volunteers, adding that only strong swimmers need apply. The response staggered him. They were worn out and tried to the limit, but one man in every three stepped out. He divided them into three groups so they could work in short spells and, when a lifeline had been rigged, led the first of them over the side.

It was tough going and needed a lot of faith, but pushing against the bow and swimming with all their strength they got her round and headed south in the end.

And now as Stan had predicted she picked up speed a little; but even so she still wasn't moving fast enough to make a course and though she never quite came up beam on to the wind again, her head was constantly swinging off one way or the other.

They had the answer now, however, and kept her going through the night with the swimming parties taking it in turn to perform the function of the inadequate rudder.

At dawn, the sea ahead was still empty and the southern horizon unbroken. They had eaten the last of their food the day before, and Sergeant Prosser was hanging on to the final meager ration of water. But the breeze was stronger and still held northerly. Seeming to draw strength and hope from the feel of it in their tousled hair and beards, they carried on.

Then, at sundown when they were stiffening themselves to face another night of it, Stan, staring through the binoculars, picked up a faint shadow low down on the skyline ahead. He said nothing about it at first, thinking it might be his eyes or imagination playing him up. But it stayed put and hardened and when he was sure, he laid back his head and spread the glad news.

"Land ahead!" he shouted hoarsely. "We've made it!"

They had, too, though it was six long weary hours later when Stan ran her up in the darkness on to a shelving beach. A party under Sergeant Steadman immediately went ashore to search for water and Josser took off on his own, aiming to make contact with the British forces somewhere along the coast road when he found it. It was a pretty slim chance of either succeeding but their luck seemed to have turned again and Sergeant Steadman was back inside the hour with the news of a well nearby. Josser took longer, but he too rolled up before daybreak, having encountered a patrol based on Tobruk which was only about a dozen miles away. He announced that transport was being laid on for them at sunup.

So in the dawn Stan stood between Josser and Joe and watched the N.C.O.'s line the men up on the beach. It was June 8th. One hundred and fifty-six hours had passed since they pushed off from Gavdopula with nothing much to go on but their everlasting guts and the will to be free. They had looked like a bunch of scarecrows then and now, after six days and seven nights aboard the old scow, they were more tattered and unkempt than ever, wasted and hollow-cheeked with hunger and thirst; but dauntless still and the light of their unbreakable spirit gleaming brightly in their sunken eyes. As they slung their rifles and moved off somebody in front started a song. One by one the men picked it up, their voices hoarse and wavering at first but quickly steadying and growing in volume.

"Waltzing Matilda, waltzing Matilda,
    You come a'waltzing Matilda with me. . . ."

The song reminded Stan first of Roo and Elena, then of the Skipper and he wondered how they were all making out. He had a strong feeling the Aussie and the girl would come through; but he wasn't so sure about the Skipper and all he could do was hope the period of captivity would be neither too long nor too harsh for him.

He turned then for a last look at the landing craft. Rusty, battered, unwieldy and unlovely, she had tried them to the limit; but he had sailed her, worked her through wind and sea, fought with her and for her, and scow though she was, it saddened him a little to leave her there to rot. After all, she had served them well in the end.

"Come on!" said Josser impatiently. "Or we'll miss the perishing bus!"

And with a little sigh, not trusting himself to speak, Stan fell in beside him and together they hurried after the marching column.